# LET THE BEAT DROP

## Cheri Ritz

**Other Bella Books by Cheri Ritz**

*Vacation People*

## About the Author

Cheri Ritz is a sucker for a good romance, so writing some happily ever after to share with the world is a dream come true! She enjoys attending her sons' many activities, volunteering with a local LGBT film festival, and spending cozy weekends marathoning TV shows. She lives in a suburb of Pittsburgh, Pennsylvania with her girlfriend, three sons, and the Sweetest Cat in the World.

# LET THE BEAT DROP

## Cheri Ritz

BELLA
BOOKS
2020

Bella Books, Inc.
P.O. Box 10543
Tallahassee, FL 32302

Printed in the United States of America on acid-free paper.

First Bella Books Edition 2020

Editor: Ann Roberts
Cover Designer: Pol Robinson

ISBN: 978-1-64247-155-7

# Acknowledgments

A great big thank you to Jessica and Linda Hill and all of the fine folks at Bella Books. You are supportive and wonderful, and I appreciate all the magic you do to make our stories happen. Thank you also to my editor Ann Roberts who took my story about two hometown girls and really made it rock! You make the process a pleasure and I learn more from you with each revision.

Writing can be a solitary experience, so I am especially grateful for my Bella author family, my author friends, and the lesfic community (both irl and in the Twitterverse!) And, of course, the readers—your kind words and excitement for stories make a writer's world go 'round.

So many people have cheered me on along the way to getting Jess & Sadie's story on the page. Thank you to JoAnn, Michelle, Philomena, and Suzy who were always quick with a pep talk or a shout out, and sometimes even a spiked slushie.

To my boys, thank you for hanging in there when I have my nose in a notebook, my head in the clouds, and I'm serving appetizers for dinner (again). You guys keep me hopping and laughing through it all.

I wrote a lot of words in this book and even a couple songs. Jaime, you were the inspiration behind it all. I really am *much more me when I'm with you*, and I wouldn't have it any other way. When finding the perfect word or filling plot holes sends me into a pattern of deep sighing and hair pulling, your quick wit and unwavering support gets me through it every time. You're the rock to my roll and I love you for it.

## Dedication

To my sisters Patty and Jen who are always quick to share a glass of wine and a good book.

# CHAPTER ONE

Sadie DuChamp had never felt less rock 'n' roll than she did that morning. She climbed the stairs to her brownstone with her bandmates, reeking of stale all-night diner coffee and bacon grease. Her band, Sugar Stix, was officially breaking up, and she could practically see her rock star dreams slipping through her black nail-polished fingertips.

Paz, their lead singer, had signed a recording contract to go solo two days earlier leaving them high and dry, scrambling to rework their Saturday night set with each of the others filling in on vocals. It had been a disaster of a show.

Then as the final nail in the band's coffin, Jason announced at their hangover helper greasy breakfast the remaining members of Sugar Stix were being evicted from the three-bedroom home he had talked his dad into renting to them at a generously discounted rate. According to Jason, his dad had no faith in the band without Paz, and he wanted them out by the end of the week so he could get paying customers in. "Money talks" was the actual phrase Jason had used.

"What are we supposed to do now?" Kellie, their bass player, followed Jason into the house trying to hold it together. She was clearly on the brink of losing it big-time. "We could all rent an apartment and pile in, even if it's close quarters. There's only four of us now. But we won't be able to book any more gigs until we replace Paz. And no gigs means no rent money. So there's that. Oh, God."

Sadie slumped down onto the arm of the couch, defeated. The thought of cramming into some tiny apartment with three other people made her want to poke her eyes out with her drumsticks. As it was, her love affair with the underground rock scene in the city had been waning for the past few months. It was late nights with low pay, and her musical ability didn't get nearly as much attention as her ripped up T-shirt and short shorts did. Hardly the glamorous picture people painted when they said the words "rock star." The additional drama with her bandmates wasn't doing anything to win her over either. They would have to come up with a hell of a solution to keep her on board this sinking ship.

"Maybe…" Jason stopped moving and Kellie walked right into him. Her gum-cracking, shadowing act appeared to be getting on his nerves. He cracked his knuckles as he spoke to her, a habit that made all his bandmates cringe. His words were slow as if that would help her understand his point. "You should have thought of that before you broke up with Paz."

"He *cheated* on me with some groupie slut after one of our shows. I *walked in* on them. The breakup's on him." Kellie squinted her eyes and rubbed her chin where it had met Jason's back.

Jason shook his head. "Whatever. But you better start packing. My dad's not dicking around. He will kick our asses out on the street." Spinning on his trainers, he stalked off to his bedroom, slamming the door behind him, obviously done with the conversation.

There were tears in Kellie's eyes as she slowly turned around. Shoulders slumped, she swiped at the dampness on her face, smearing the mascara already snaking down her cheeks. Sadie's heart went out to her. Paz had been a total douche canoe to her the whole time they dated. And that wasn't the first time he had cheated on her. Just the first time she had caught him. Although Sadie was in no position to judge—her last attempt at romance had blown up spectacularly as well. At least Sadie's ex had had the good sense to never bother her again even though she had it on good authority that he was still working his day job at the adult bookstore a few blocks away.

"Come on." She spread her arms open and gestured for her friend to fold into them. Her body fell against her with a heaving sob that bubbled up out of her. "No one is blaming you for Sugar Stix breaking up, Kel. Jason is just butt hurt and embarrassed that his dad is making him move out of the house and be financially responsible for once in his life. Don't listen to him."

Even as she said it, Jason started yelling from his bedroom, a string of unintelligible shouts and cries that she assumed had to be cuss words based on his tone. That was confirmed when he opened his bedroom door again. "Where the fuck is my motherfucking guitar?" He bellowed in the girls' direction.

Sadie squinted eye daggers at him. "How the hell would we know? Where did you leave it?"

Jason wasn't exactly the picture of responsibility, which shouldn't have surprised anyone considering the way his father had bailed him out of any tight spot he ever got himself into.

"I'm serious," he continued. "It's gone. Like, not here."

"Yes. I caught that when you said *gone*." Sadie continued to glare at him. The guys in the house were really starting to piss her off. They had all gotten along for over a year, practicing, playing gigs, living together day in and day out, then one thing went wrong and they had all fallen apart. Well, two things. But still.

"Well, where the hell is it?" he screamed as if he was accusing the girls of wrongdoing, which, needless to say, didn't sit well with either of them.

Kellie slipped out of Sadie's arms and faced him, her spirit suddenly restored. Her gaze was hard even through the red tinge in her eyes from crying. "Jason, this is not our problem. It's yours. You weren't too concerned about helping us solve the living situation, so you can figure it out yourself."

"Someone's gotta know!" he shouted back, loud enough to roust a sleepy-faced Jon, the other member of their group, out of his bedroom.

"What. The. Hell," Jon growled, rubbing his hand through his hair. "Some of us are trying to sleep."

Jon, who shared a room with Paz, had still been completely passed out when the others went to breakfast at the diner down the street. They had left him behind.

"My guitar is gone. My good one." Redness was creeping up Jason's neck along the veins that were starting to bulge there. Maybe he was going to turn into the Hulk. That would be interesting.

"Yeah, man." Jon nodded like he didn't have a care in the world. Like they were discussing the weather. "Paz and that chick stopped by while you guys were out. He grabbed the rest of his stuff. And he took your guitar. He said you owed him." He glanced at the girls. "If I were you two, I'd check your room too."

"What the fuck?" Jason spat out. "Why didn't you stop him?"

Jon shrugged. "Wasn't my shit."

Jason was in front of him in a flash, shoving him in the chest with both hands, catching him off guard and sending him backpedaling to stay on his feet. "Asshole! You just let him take our stuff? What the fuck?"

Jon recovered and swung at Jason, connecting with his jaw. Jason's whole face went beet red and he tackled Jon to the ground, throwing punches as they hit the floor.

"Stop it, you guys!" Kellie half-screeched, half-sobbed, and took a step in their direction, but Sadie grabbed her arm before she could get too close. She didn't need to get smacked for being in the line of fire. The boys could work things out between them. Sadie was much more interested in checking on her own belongings.

"Come on. We better look in our room." She pulled Kellie along with her, edging past the scrambling guys, down the hall to their own bedroom.

Unfortunately, Paz and his new girlfriend had visited their room as well. Dresser drawers had been left ajar, an indicator that someone had been in them since Sadie had a compulsive habit of making sure they were completely shut before leaving the room. She instinctively went to the top drawer and the envelope where she kept her cash, not the least bit surprised to find the five hundred dollars she had stashed there from their last several gigs was nowhere to be found. "Fuck."

Kellie was standing by the little desk in the corner of the room by her bed. Her tears had started flowing full force all over again. "My new red leather jacket. It's gone."

Losing that jacket sucked. Kellie had only worn it a few times. And now it was in the possession of the bitch who had stolen her boyfriend too. What a slap in the face. She crumpled into a sobbing blob on her bed.

Sadie felt like a total idiot for thinking she could trust these people just because they were in a band together. It was like the past sixteen months had meant nothing. Two of the guys were beating the crap out of one another. Paz had robbed them all and taken off for God-knows-where. The only one in the bunch she had any feelings for at this point was Kellie, and there was no way the two of them could continue the band without the others. She was just glad she had left her drums in her car or they would probably be gone too. There was nothing left for Sadie there. It was time to get the hell out of New York.

She pulled her phone out of her back pocket and dialed up the one person who she knew would always be glad to see her.

"Mom, I've had a change of plans. I'm moving back home."

When Sadie returned to her childhood home in Tucker Pointe less than a week later in the dead of night, nobody was there to greet her. She hadn't expected anything different when she had decided to make the trip. The last time she was home was to attend her father's funeral, and Dad had been gone nine months. She assumed Mom was already asleep, which was a very normal thing for her to be doing considering the hour. Exhausted from the journey, she didn't even bother hauling herself up the stairs to her old bedroom. She just passed out on the couch.

The bright sun streaming in through the big window in the front of the house woke Sadie the next day. The dust particles floating in the rays of light indicated the floor-length curtains might be in need of a good cleaning. That was the kind of thing Sadie would help her mother with as part of her fresh start. It was the least she could do after... Well, it was the least she could do.

With the house still quiet, she rolled off the couch and shuffled sleepily past the piano to the kitchen. She rummaged through the cupboards for what she needed to get her morning fix of caffeine, noting the place hadn't changed much since she had first moved out over a year and a half before. As the coffee gurgled, she noted a new wrought-iron table by the sofa. There was no longer an entertainment center housing the television—now it was a flat screen hung on the wall. That left the perfect spot for Sadie to set up her drum set once she brought it in from the car. She would get to that later, but first she had to know if one other thing had remained the same as she left it.

Full coffee mug in hand, she went down the steps to the game room. Her father had finished the basement when she was eight, doing much of the work himself. When the drywall was up and painted, and the carpeting had been laid, he added the finishing touches—a billiards table, dartboard, and wet bar complete with mini fridge. Sadie's favorite part of the whole basement makeover had been the two arcade video games he had purchased for her: Ms. Pac-Man and Donkey Kong. Sadie always loved video games, but it was her dad who got her hooked on the retro ones. His stories about spending hours in the local arcade as a kid, spending every quarter he could find in the house, delighted her and helped her relate to him as more than just a parent. For the first time, Sadie realized he had been a kid once too. It sparked a connection they hadn't shared before then. She fell in love with the cheesy graphics, the silly characters, and the tinny musical displays that played between levels. One of the hardest things about moving out of her parents' home had been abandoning her beloved arcade games. She was pleased to find them right where she had left them, a tether to her memories of her father, although unplugged since she last set her hands on them back before she originally left for New York.

Sadie reached behind the dusty Ms. Pac-Man machine and plugged it in, breathing a sigh of relief when the screen came alive and the cheerful theme song played. Reliable as ever. She smiled and patted it on its pink and blue side like she was greeting an old friend. Might as well test her out. She found an old rag in the adjacent laundry room and wiped the machine down, cringing at the layer of dust that had collected on the screen. The dirt clung to the blue cloth in her hand—one of her dad's old security guard T-shirts from the agency he worked for before she was born, before he started his own business. Gross. She tossed it to the floor beside the machine and hit the start button.

It was three games later when she finally took the cold contents of her mug back up to the kitchen and got a light breakfast ready for her mom. With a fresh cup of coffee and some fruit on a breakfast tray, Sadie climbed the stairs to the second floor. The big house seemed so quiet with only the two of them in it. Maybe that was how it had felt for her parents after she left for New York. She couldn't imagine what it had felt like for her mom to be rattling around all alone in the place since he died.

Sadie tiptoed into her mom's bedroom. She didn't want to startle her, but she did want to rouse her from what she suspected was an extended, depression-fueled slumber. She set the breakfast tray on the bedside table and gently ran her hand through her mom's hair. "Good morning, sleepyhead."

Her mom's eyes blinked open and a trace of a smile graced her face. "Hey, baby. I'm so glad you're home."

Sadie bent forward and kissed her head. "Me too, Mom." She meant it sincerely. She had known her mother was still struggling with grief based on their phone conversations over the past nine months, but seeing it in person was a whole new kick in the gut. Her mom was thinner and her eyes a little more sunken since her dad's funeral. Sadness had taken its toll. She should have come home to help her mother sooner. "I brought you a little something to eat. Give it a try, okay?" Before she could slide away, her mother clutched her forearm.

"You've got something new there." Her mom's gaze rested on the ink on Sadie's left shoulder. In the sleeveless black T-shirt, most of the art showed. "What's different since the last time I saw you?"

Sadie looked down at her arm, impressed that her mother could see the difference amid the collection of tattoos. She knew exactly which piece her mom was referring to, and as she spotted it, she smiled. She was especially proud of that one. It was a black bird spreading its wings to take flight. "It's the one right here. I got it after I broke up with Corey."

Her mom studied it a moment before nodding her sleepy approval. "Very pretty. You know, I never liked that boy. I think he stayed around a little too long." Her gaze rose to meet her daughter's. "I'm glad you flew free like your black bird there."

It warmed Sadie's heart that she got the meaning behind the ink. "Me too." She bent forward and kissed her mother's forehead. It was good to be home again. Guilt tugged her heartstrings. She had neglected her family for a crappy relationship and her career with a band that had imploded with the first bump they hit in the road. But now she was home and she would do her damnedest to make up for that. She would help her mom get back on her feet—no matter what. "Mom, I've decided I'm gonna stay in town for a year and kind of regroup. That way I'll be here to help you out while you get your equilibrium, or whatever, back. It will be good for both of us."

"Sadie, you don't have to do that."

"I know I don't have to." She had to try to make things up to her mom. The idea was ballooning inside her. She felt lighter already. "I want to."

While her mom ate breakfast, Sadie dragged her drum kit in from the car and reassembled it in the corner of the family room. Then she stuck her earbuds in, pulled up a playlist of covers Sugar Stix used to do, and drummed along.

She got lost in the music, pounding out her feelings about Sugar Stix breaking up, imagining punching Paz in the nose for stealing her money, and beating down her guilt about the pit of grief her mother had fallen into while she'd been away. Bobbing her head along to the song, Sadie hummed the melody and let the joy of making music carry her to her bliss. She had just hit the last cymbal crash of the song when she noticed she was no longer alone in the living room.

Gasping, she dropped one stick and almost fell backward off her stool, but her shock dissolved into giggles as her mother's friends, Sophie, Marley, and Kristen waved from where they stood across the room holding Tupperware containers of food and coupon fliers from the newspaper.

Sadie yanked her earbuds out by the cord and ran her hands through her short hair as she greeted them with hugs all around. "What are you all doing here?"

"Sadie DuChamp, you're back!" Sophie set her belongings down on the kitchen table, freeing her arms to give Sadie a proper squeeze before looking her over. "Aren't you a sight? You're reminding me of my days making music out on the road. Those were good days. I bet your mother is thrilled to have you here."

Sadie beamed. As hard as it was to give up on Sugar Stix and her rock 'n' roll dreams in New York, it really was good to be home in so many other ways. Her mother's group of neighborhood friends was something she had truly missed.

"We could hear you playing from outside, so we let ourselves in." Kristen dangled a set of keys in the air. Her short blond hair was spikey, same as Sadie remembered it. "It's coupon swapping day. We do it every Sunday over brunch," she explained. "Where's your mother?"

Sadie nodded toward the staircase in the front hall. "Still upstairs as far as I know." She shrugged and grinned sheepishly. "I guess I was a little distracted by my music. I'll go tell her you're all here."

To her surprise when she got upstairs, her mom was out of bed and had even changed into yoga pants and a long, light knit powder-blue sweater. Still not her usual look, but a big step up from the old, tattered pajamas she had worn earlier that morning. Downstairs, the ladies had already set up a buffet of various salads they had brought along. The women were seated around the kitchen table, coupon fliers and scissors laid out in front of them.

Her mother went to retrieve the Sunday paper someone had brought in for her. "Sadie, come fix yourself a plate. You can sit with us and visit."

She sat down next to Sophie, who looked put together as ever, her dark hair in a tight knot on the back of her head, bright poppy print sundress with a light sweater on her shoulders, and her signature bright red lipstick.

"So the band went kaput?" Sophie's dark-penciled eyebrows bunched together as she patted Sadie's hand sympathetically. "I'm sorry."

"Something like that." Sadie nodded. She appreciated the kindness. "Thank you. I'll find something else."

She did need to find something else, at least temporarily while staying in Tucker Pointe for the next year, something to keep her busy and give her income. She would look into that later. It wasn't like she was going to find a job on a Sunday.

The women chattered away, trading coupons with each other and eating salad. Her mom was much more reserved than Sadie had ever seen her be with her friends, and she picked at her food, but at least she was participating. It was a step in the right direction.

As the exchange wore down, the women stacked their coupons and stashed them in envelopes or plastic organizers. Sadie leaned back in her chair, belly full on homemade food. She had spent way too long existing on takeout and ramen noodles. The unexpected feast had been a welcome change for her.

Kristen snapped the elastic in place on her coupon organizer and asked, "Marley, isn't Jessica coming home from school soon?"

"She is." Marley's grin was almost bigger than her gigantic boobs. Almost. "She's due at the end of the week and I can hardly wait. I'm so excited to have my baby home."

Jess Moran was no baby, and it was no secret that she was her mother's whole world. Sadie remembered her from high school, although Jess had been a couple grades ahead of her. Even though she lived down the street, they never mixed and mingled back then. Jess was in with the preppy, jock types. Sadie was quite comfortable in the artsy crowd. But anytime they crossed paths in the neighborhood, Jess always seemed nice enough.

"Is she coming home alone for the summer?" Sophie, who prided herself on always being on top of the neighborhood scuttlebutt, cut to the chase and flat-out asked. "Is she dating anyone?"

"Oh, you know Jess, such a free spirit. Sometimes I wonder if she'll ever settle down." Marley pressed her lips together and shook her head. "I don't worry about it. She's so busy with school now. There will be plenty of time for serious romance later. I'm just glad I get to have her around for the whole summer."

"It's nice to have our kids come back." Her mom rested her arm on the back of Sadie's chair and gave her shoulder a loving squeeze.

"We got a little concert when we walked in." Marley grinned. "I can see why you're so proud of this one, Jennifer."

The compliment made her mom smile, which in turn made Sadie smile. "Sadie, play something now that I'm down here."

"Mom, it's drums. It won't sound like an actual song."

"I'll play along with you," Marley proposed, nodding in the direction of the guitars in the corner of the living room.

"You play?" How could Sadie not know that one of her mother's dearest friends was a musician?

Marley laughed. "I do. I even sing."

"Well, let's go." Sadie hopped out of her seat. It had been less than a week, but she missed playing with others so much, she didn't want to give Marley the chance to back out. "What should we play?"

Marley looped the guitar strap over her shoulder and tested the strings. Sadie didn't know how long the guitar had sat untouched, but it still sounded relatively in tune. "'Runaround Sue.' You know that one?"

Sadie gave a nod and twirled a stick around her fingers like a baton. "That's a rock standard. Let's do it."

She clicked her sticks, counting them in, and Marley strummed and sang. Her speaking voice tended to be on the squeaky side, so Sadie was pleasantly surprised when Marley's singing voice came out melodious and on point.

By the second verse, Sophie had joined in singing harmony and Kristen was picking out the tune on the piano. When they hit the chorus again, even Sadie's mom had picked up the other guitar and was singing along, a hint of her old sparkle in her eyes. As Marley strummed the last chord and Sadie pounded out a flashy ending to the song, a plan to distract her mother from her grief began to form in Sadie's mind.

# CHAPTER TWO

Jess Moran stretched her sleepy body, blinked her eyes against the morning sun peeking through the edges of the window blinds, and slowly untangled herself from the snoring girl in her bed. She grabbed the cargo shorts she'd worn the night before from the floor and slipped them on as she tiptoed out of the room. The apartment smelled like frying bacon. *Cassie to the rescue.*

"Hey, Sleeping Beauty, I thought you would be on the road by now." Her roommate Cassie stood in front of the ancient avocado green stove in their low-rent student housing apartment and waved her spatula dramatically as she spoke. "I made some breakfast. There's enough for your sleepy girlfriend in there too." The way her unruly red curls poked out of her messy bun gave her a bit of a mad scientist effect.

So, Cassie hadn't missed their late-night return to the apartment. That late night was the reason Jess hadn't been up and on her way home as early as expected. She'd given in to exhaustion and overslept.

"Yeah, her." Jess winced as she glanced back over her shoulder at the bedroom door. "She's not my girlfriend. Hell, I don't even know her name."

"Jessica Rose Moran," Cassie scolded, still waving that damn spatula. "You slept with some drunken undergrad whose name you don't even know?"

"I didn't sleep with her." Jess rolled her eyes at her roommate's dramatics and grabbed a bottle of orange juice from the fridge. "When we left the party last night, I had no idea how drunk she was. I was going to walk her home, but she was so smashed she couldn't even tell me where she lived. I didn't know what to do with her. I brought her back here and put her to bed, but absolutely nothing happened between us. Give me a little credit please."

Cassie finished plating breakfast and brought two dishes full of scrambled eggs and bacon to their tiny kitchen table. "I'd like to give you a lot of credit, but the seemingly endless parade of women you've marched through our apartment this school year suggests you haven't earned the credit."

Jess wasted no time digging in to her breakfast. She hadn't had nearly as much to drink at the party as the girl still snoozing in her bed, but she had consumed enough alcohol that the thought of some greasy bacon in her stomach was a glorious and much welcomed proposition. "I feel like we've had this conversation before. I'm a busy gal. I have school. I have work. I don't have a lot of time left over for romantic pursuits."

"Right. It's all about time management and not at all about your unwillingness to open up to anybody."

"I'm a very private person. I keep to myself. There's nothing wrong with that." She shrugged and shut the conversation down. "So anyway, once I get Siesta Susan out of here, I'm gonna hit the road. Jeep's all packed."

Cassie stabbed at the eggs on her plate with her fork. "You packed up everything before you went to the party last night?"

"Everything but the sheets on my bed." Jess couldn't hide her excited grin. "I really wanted to get an early start. I'm surprising my mom. She's not expecting me until tomorrow."

"You're such a mama's girl," Cassie teased as she threw a balled-up paper napkin across the table at her. "You know, you would have your master's degree already if you would stay at school and take classes instead of going home for the summer."

Cassie had a whole different perspective on their current educational situations. She was a medical research student. She would be attending year-round until her team produced something worthy of a medical journal. She barely took a break from the lab for a good night's sleep, much less a whole summer off.

"Well, the family business calls. My mom needs me to work for her at Queen of Hearts. I'm heading up all of the social media now, plus summer is our busy season." Jess's heart swelled with pride at the mention of the company her mother had built from the ground up, all the while raising her alone. Cassie had hit the mark when she called Jess a mama's girl, and Jess wasn't ashamed of that one bit. She had always helped her mom with her craft vodka business, and with the twentieth anniversary celebration for Queen of Hearts coming up this summer, she would be needed more than ever. "Besides, I enjoy the time with her. It's always been the two of us making our way through this world, and we're a hell of a team."

"The way you'll have your eyes glued to that phone I don't know how you have time to enjoy anything. When it comes to social media, you really are the queen."

"Only when it comes to the family biz." Jess frowned. "When it comes to that stuff, my mom is completely clueless. She still refers to the hashtag as a 'pound sign.' Like I said, she needs me."

"I know, but I miss you when you're not here." Cassie reached across the table and gave Jess's hand a squeeze. "I mean, you can always make it up to me by bringing back some of that Queen of Hearts vodka at the end of summer."

"Oh my God, please don't say the V word." A small, raspy voice came from the direction of Jess's room.

Jess's bedmate appeared in the doorway. To Jess's relief, the woman had her clothes and flip-flops on and appeared to be ready to make her exit. Jess got up from the table in an effort to be a good host right down to the bitter end. "Oh, hey. Good morning. Did you want some breakfast?"

"No thanks. I'm gonna go." The girl pushed her messy brown hair out of her eyes and crossed the room to the front door. Jess followed her to usher her out. Before leaving, she paused and said, "Uh, did I have sex with one of you last night?"

"No," they both responded without hesitation.

"Okay. Cool." She shrugged and addressed Jess. "Anyway, thanks for letting me crash here. You want to do something tomorrow night?"

"I'm actually leaving town for a couple of months." Jess had never been so glad to have a ready-made excuse right at hand.

The undergrad turned to Cassie next. "How about you?"

"No thanks." Cassie continued to clear the table without even looking up as she declined the offer. "I'm straight."

Jess shook her head and bit her lip to keep from laughing at Cassie's flippant reply, but the hungover girl seemed unaffected. "Cool. See you guys around."

Jess shut the door behind her and leaned her back against it, finally letting out a laugh. "*I'm straight?* Very smooth."

"Well, it's true." Cassie finished wiping the table and said, "I didn't want to lead her on, unlike you, bringing a date back here and then not putting out."

"Ha, ha." Jess sidled up to Cassie at the sink and dried the dishes. "I'll say it one more time: that chick was not my date. I was trying to help. I have no interest in being with a woman who was too sloppy drunk to even remember what happened the night before."

It was the truth in this case, but as she sunk back into her chair at the kitchen table to finish her juice, Jess couldn't shake Cassie's words earlier about her unwillingness to open up to people and let them in. She couldn't deny that there were parts of her life she preferred to keep private. Hell, she and Cassie had been friends for almost five years and even Cassie didn't know some things about her. Sometimes that was just the way it had to be.

Some secrets were meant to remain untold.

# CHAPTER THREE

Tuesday afternoon, after securing a part-time job waiting tables at Lenny's Pizza Parlor, Sadie sat poolside with Marley. She had a plan to help her mom get back to her old self, but there was no way she could do it alone. She would need Marley and the neighborhood salad-sharing gang to help. "You know the other day, when we were singing after the coupon thingy?"

Marley nodded. "It was fun." Her blue eyes sparkled when she smiled. "You're very good."

"Thanks. You were awesome too." Heat rushed to Sadie's cheeks at the compliment. As many gigs as she had played behind Sugar Stix, she wasn't used to playing in front of people who really knew her or receiving compliments from them. But she did appreciate it. "By the time we finished the song, my mom had picked up her guitar and joined in."

"She did, didn't she?" Marley looked pensive, her eyebrows pushed low. "She does love music. One night the cul-de-sac gang all went out for karaoke and…" It was Marley's turn to blush, clearly remembering a wild night shared among friends. "Well, anyway, that's where you get it from."

"Yeah. Duh." Sadie smiled. "I started thinking that maybe it was something that might get her out and about again. At least a little."

"Huh." Marley sucked on the reusable straw in her cucumber water. Maybe proper hydration was why she looked so young. "You could be on to something. Me and the gals have been looking for excuses to drag Jennifer out of bed, but not anything that would be too much of a push for her. She needs time to work through her feelings. She needs to take the time and grieve. That's a natural part of life. We've all experienced loss in one way or another, so we have an idea of what she's going through."

"A group that gets together to play music and socialize could be that kind of thing," Sadie reasoned. "It's her closest friends, and it wouldn't entail getting dolled up or going out in actual public. Very low pressure."

"You want us to start a band? Like, a rock band?"

Sadie's cheeks flushed hot again. It sounded kind of silly when she said it like that, but basically that was what she was suggesting. She nervously rubbed the metal ring in her eyebrow. "Yeah. I guess that's what I'm saying. Just for fun," she added quickly.

A wide smile lit up Marley's face and her eyes flashed with excitement. Marley was a beautiful woman, who, even though she was in her forties, could easily pass for ten years younger, especially when her expression brightened that way.

"I have something I need to show you," she said. "Come on."

Sadie followed her into the immaculately clean kitchen, which was decorated in a French country wine theme with iron light fixtures and distressed cabinets. Marley led her down the basement stairs. The stairway was dark but carpeted, and when they reached the bottom, Marley clicked on the overhead lighting revealing a large, finished space that served as a rec room. There was an overstuffed sectional couch in one area facing a wall-mounted television. Beyond that was a drum set, several guitars and practice amps, and a keyboard. There was even a microphone propped on a stand. Basically everything you needed for a band.

"Ta-da!" She spread her arms with a flourish, laughing as she beamed at Sadie. "I thought this stuff would rot from neglect down here and now it has a chance at a second life."

"What the heck? Are you in some kind of secret band I don't know about? Where did all this stuff come from?"

Marley continued to laugh, obviously pleased with Sadie's delighted reaction. "Jess and her friends used to play around with it all the time down here when she lived at home." She shrugged. "I never got rid of it after she went away to college."

How could she have not known that Marley's daughter was a musician? They went to the same high school. Surely their musical paths would have crossed at some point. "My mind is blown. Jess was in a band?"

"Don't be too impressed. They thought they were a band. Truth was they stank. But they had a lot of fun down here fooling around." She had that wistful look in her eye that parents got when they talked about things their kids used to do. "Maybe we can put this stuff to use again? If you need my help, I'm in."

Sadie walked over to the drums and rapped her knuckles on the surface of the snare. "Do you think Sophie and Kristen will do it? I mean, I've heard Sophie's stories about playing bass in a band back in the day, and Kristen seems like she knows her way around a piano."

Marley gently put her hand on Sadie's shoulder. "Jennifer is one of our dearest friends. If this helps her, I'm sure we'll all be happy to do it. I'll call the group and invite them for coffee tomorrow. We can start then."

"Thanks, Marley." A weight had been lifted off Sadie's chest.

"Sure thing. Now come on, let's get back to soaking in the sun while we have the chance." Marley marched her back up the stairs to the kitchen. "Feel free to hop in the pool if you need to cool down. I'll be back out in a few."

Sadie headed back outside with light, quick steps across the burning hot cement surface of the patio that connected the house and the pool. The bright sun dancing across the surface of the water beckoned to her. She didn't even spare a second thought before slipping out of her shorts and tank, down to her bikini and diving into the deep end.

She pulled her arms through the water and glided along, the motion testing her shoulders, her muscles working in a way they hadn't in a long time. She had been a regular at the gym when she lived at home, but once she had moved to New York, Sadie couldn't afford it, along with daily coffee from the big-name shop and purchasing every new shade of nail polish that her favorite brand unveiled.

While she was in the band, her muscle strength routine consisted mainly of hauling equipment to and from gigs. It was enough to keep her arms defined and looking decent in tank tops, so she couldn't complain. But maybe the gym routine was something to revisit while she was staying with her mom in Tucker Pointe.

When she reached the far end of the pool, she submerged her whole head, diving down under the surface, filling herself with that weird, muffled underwater version of silence. It was refreshing and centering, and gave her a sense of peace.

As her body sliced through the water her mind drifted into thoughts of the summer. She was glad to be home with her mother, and she'd be fine for a year, but she didn't intend to stick around in Tucker Pointe forever. Getting Marley on board with her plan had been a good first step to taking care of business, but Sadie still needed to figure out what she was doing career-wise, post Sugar Stix. She was grateful to have work at Lenny's, but eventually she would need goals for something more permanent.

The repetition of the back and forth laps of the pool was perfect for getting lost in her thoughts, and Sadie allowed them to churn about as she swam as if perhaps they would resolve themselves on their own. She imagined she was batting her problems away with each pull of her arms, and for a moment she was able to let go and relax. Until she came up for air and saw Jess Moran, Marley's daughter, standing on the pool deck watching her, arms crossed, a wry grin on her face, and much more devastatingly gorgeous than she had been in high school.

*Damn.*

"Didn't mean to interrupt," Jess called across the pool. Her eyebrow arched as she looked Sadie over. "I thought my mother would be out here."

"She's in the house," Sadie answered quickly, kind of wanting her to leave, sort of wanting her to keep talking. She slicked her hair back with her hands and hoped she didn't look as off-balance as she felt. She bit her bottom lip and tasted chlorine before flutter kicking over to the side where the other girl was standing. If they were going to continue the conversation, there was no need to shout it out for the whole subdivision to hear.

Jess's posture relaxed and she slid her hands into the pockets of her cargo shorts, uncovering the Cinci Heart Foundation Fun Run logo on her faded green T-shirt. She still owned the girl next door look—long blond hair, fresh-faced with a light sprinkling of freckles. Still with the same striking aquamarine eyes and large, sexy mouth.

*Wait. Was her mouth always that sexy?*

Sadie rested her elbows on the deck of the pool, propping herself up, and tried to look cool, calm and collected despite her hammering heartbeat. Jess's gaze slid down to the tattoo on her shoulder. "I didn't know you were home. Your mom said I could use the pool. We were, uh, working on something."

"I just pulled in. She wasn't even expecting me today. I wanted to surprise her, you know?" Her kind smile made it clear that she was excited to see her mother, and Sadie liked that about Jess. A lot of her friends acted like they were "too cool" to treat their parents with respect. "So, what brings the local rock star back to town?"

"Rock star?" Sadie laughed. Her hole-in-the-wall bar gigs with Sugar Stix barely paid for food to eat and hardly qualified her for rock star status. She couldn't tell if Jess was being ironic or not, and she wasn't exactly ready to spill her guts on the truth of the band's breakup with a woman she barely knew, so she went with a diversion tactic. "That's an awfully personal question for someone who hasn't spoken to me since the last high school pep rally she attended."

"Ah." Jess grinned and rocked back on her heels. "The pre-graduation pep rally. Principal Boyle really knocked that speech out of the park. Who could forget it?" She was definitely teasing that time and Sadie appreciated the pass on answering the original question.

She laughed and went along with it. "Well, he was one hell of an administrator."

"That he was. That he was." Jess nodded solemnly, keeping her expression even except the one side of her mouth that hitched up like some laughter could sneak out at any moment. She coyly ducked her head and when their gazes met again her expression had shifted to much more sincere. Her bright eyes shone with the reflection of the sun shining off the water and Sadie's breath caught at how beautiful they were, but then Jess spoke again, breaking the spell. "I guess I better go find my mom. But it was nice to see you again, rock star."

She tried not to wince at the nickname. "Yeah. You too. I'll get out of your pool and head home."

"Don't leave on my account. Stay as long as you like. You won't bother me any." Jess winked before turning and heading into the house.

Sadie continued to hang on the edge of the pool and watch Jess walk away. The back view of her in those cargo shorts was equally attractive as the front, and her calf muscles had some serious definition. Probably from entering 5k fun runs for charities. Jess Moran had grown into a fine-looking woman. If Sadie wasn't still on the dating hiatus she decided she needed after her ugly relationship with Corey, she might have considered Jess date-worthy. But romance was the last thing she needed with the mess on her hands at home. So a few outdated jabs at their old high school principal was as far as the thing between them was gonna go.

*That was little Sadie DuChamp from down the street? Holy hell.* Jess stepped into the air-conditioned coolness of her mother's house and swiped at the beads of sweat on her forehead with the back of her hand. She suspected it was more than the noon sun that had her overheated. The last time she had laid eyes on

Sadie she had been a little, artsy-fartsy freshman who happened to live in the same neighborhood. Now she looked more like… well, a rock star.

She cringed, remembering that she had spoken the term out loud to Sadie. But it fit her perfectly. The short, auburn hair slicked back from the pool water, the eyebrow piercing, the toned arms, and damn, those tattoos. The woman was sexy as fuck. Maybe that was what getting out of the Midwest and moving to New York did to a person. Or maybe the time spent chasing her dreams had served her that well. Whatever it was, it had worked. Sadie was hot as hell and Jess had immediately fallen under her spell.

Jess shook her head, pulling herself out of the Sadie DuChamp daydream fog. She needed to push the thought of flirting with Sadie out of her mind. She was in town to spend time with her mom, help with her company, and get some useful, real-world business experience. Not to date or get wrapped up in silly romantic fantasies about the pretty girl who lived down the street. Hell, for all Jess knew, Sadie was totally straight anyway. She sure didn't have time to be chasing some straight girl crush.

She fished her car keys out of her pocket and tossed them onto the granite top of the kitchen island before grabbing a cold bottle of water from the fridge. "Mom, where are you?" she called in between sips.

"Baby, is that you?" Her mom's excited voice—the one that slid up about two octaves higher than her regular voice—echoed from the next room. Her mom bounded around the corner and wrapped her up in a big bear hug. "I wasn't expecting you today."

Jess inhaled the familiar flowery scent of her mom's perfume as she squeezed her right back. She was glad to be home. "Well, I couldn't wait any longer to get our summer started. I missed you."

"I missed you too." Her mom let her go and took a step back to give her a good once-over. "Oh, sweetie, I'm so happy you're here. We're going to have a great summer. We've got lots of great Queen of Hearts events lined up and the twentieth anniversary gala to top it all off."

"Sounds incredible."

Jess smiled at her mom's enthusiasm for her business. It was that energy that made Queen of Hearts vodka the successful venture that it was. She was proud of the company, and she was honored to get to be a part of it as she finished her education and worked toward becoming her mom's business partner.

"Of course there will still be plenty of time to lounge around the pool as well." Her hand flew up to her bright pink lips and her eyebrows shot up in alarm. "The pool! I left Sadie DuChamp out there swimming. I told her I'd be right back out, and then I got distracted when I heard you come in."

*Sadie DuChamp out in the backyard...pulling herself up out of the pool with those toned, muscled shoulders...dripping wet as she stood in the sunshine...finally toweling off as she shook the water from her short hair...*

Yeah, she was going to have to stop the fantasizing about the neighbor or it was going to be one long summer. Hoping her expression didn't betray her unwholesome thoughts, Jess slipped a hair tie off her wrist and pulled her long hair up into a knot. "Um, I think Sadie was heading home when I came in. Actually, I might have scared her off."

"You did what? Oh, Jess." Her mom rushed over to the French doors and surveyed the pool through the glass panes. "Yep, she's gone. Why did you scare her off? What did you do?"

"I didn't mean to." She shrugged and played with the cap of her water bottle, too ashamed to meet her mother's gaze. She didn't need to flirt with Sadie when she saw her in the pool. She could have said hello like a normal person and gone on her way. But instead, her old habits got the best of her—see a pretty woman, ratchet up the charm to maximum impact. "I hadn't been expecting to run into her there. She kind of caught me off guard." That was the truth.

"Sadie came home from New York last weekend. Her band broke up, and she's not sure what her next move is. She's got a lot going on right now." Her mom spun around quickly and clapped her hands together. "You know, that girl could probably use a friend around here. Maybe you could hang out with her?"

Could she hang out with a woman who sent her flirt instinct into overdrive and manage to behave as just friends? It would be a hell of a way to spend her free time, a real exercise in self-restraint. Of course, if Sadie was straight anyway, she might not even know she was sending Jess's hormones into a frenzy, and she may not think anything at all of Jess's flirtations. Being friends might not be a totally impossible task. She could do it. She could be friends with Sadie DuChamp. "Yeah, sure, Mom. I can do that."

"She's a sweet girl, and she's got loads of style." She clapped her hands several times in a row, her signal for an exciting idea. "Oh my gosh, what if the two of you hit it off and you start dating? You would make an adorable couple!"

To her embarrassment, Jess's cheeks flushed hot at the suggestion of being part of a couple with Sadie. "Mom, I agreed to friends—nothing more. Besides, Sadie isn't gay."

"Hmm. No, that's not right. She was in a relationship with a guy about six months ago, but I'm certain that Jennifer mentioned she was dating a girl at some point before that."

*Great.* This arrangement was turning into risky business really fast. The woman who had gone from girl down the street to rock star, and given Jess a bad case of the tingles in her nether region with a flash of her smile, was definitely on the "hands off" list. Their moms were practically best friends. Jess's mom was acting like she was Sadie's biggest fan. There was no way getting involved with this girl in a romantic capacity could end well. It was all too messy. She wouldn't be able to deal with her mom's disappointment if things went south between them. But hanging around with Sadie and keeping her hands to herself was going to be a hell of a task, especially now that there was a real chance Sadie might flirt back.

Her mom was still posed with her hands clasped together, that happy, hopeful expression on her face, waiting for Jess to respond.

"Friends, Mom," Jess sighed. "Just friends."

# CHAPTER FOUR

"Marley is *amazing*, Mom." Sadie sat on the edge of her mom's bed where she had found her when she got back from swimming at the Morans' house. Based on the drawn blinds and rumpled bed, her mom had been there all morning. "I had a nice time catching up with her. You should have come too." Sadie would use any excuse to get her up and moving. That would be her new objective.

Her mom seemed to ignore that last part, but at least she was smiling. "You thought she was all pretty face and big, fake boobs, didn't you?"

"Mom!" Sadie's cheeks flushed hot, not because her mother had talked about her friend's fake boobs, but because she had been called out on exactly what she had assumed about the bleach-bottle blond. Sometimes appearances were deceiving. Lesson learned.

"Did you know her company had the top-selling craft vodka in the country last year?"

"What? Queen of Hearts?" Sadie chewed on her bottom lip and digested the new information.

"Yes. And Marley built that company from the ground up." Her mom nodded, eyebrows raised in a "Don't judge a book by its cover" expression. "They make a bunch of gourmet-flavored vodkas, and that's what's set her apart. Flavors like Maple Bacon and Mocha Espresso."

"Maple Bacon vodka?" Sadie scrunched up her face in disgust. "Who would drink that?"

"Apparently plenty of people. It's one of their most popular flavors." Her mom sat up and pushed back to lean against the headboard. It was as if the conversation about her friend was bringing her to life. "What did you think her company did all these years?"

"I don't know, made regular, plain old vodka?" Truth was Sadie had never really thought about it. She knew Marley was a single mom. Jess's father hadn't been in the picture since the two of them had moved in to the neighborhood when Sadie was in middle school. Marley was in Mom's circle of friends, and she owned a company that made vodka. That was pretty much it. "I didn't think at all. She's really cool, though. Oh, and she asked me to remind you about her party next Saturday night. You're going to go, right?"

Her mom picked at the edge of the bedsheet. Stalling. "I'll go for at least some of it. I don't want to let Marley down."

The neighborhood party would be the perfect occasion to get her mom out of the house. Her friend circle would be there, so a certain level of comfort was guaranteed, plus Sadie would be there to keep an eye on her as well. It was the perfect social event to work into her "Get Mom Back Out in The World" plan. Baby steps were definitely the way to go.

"We'll go together. It will be fun," Sadie promised, but when her mom's expression fell to a half smile that didn't reach her eyes, Sadie second-guessed the prediction.

That familiar rush of guilt filled her, making her pulse pound in her neck. Sadie had been in such a hurry to get back to New York City and Sugar Stix after her father passed that she never even stopped to think about how much her mother might need her to stay at home with her for a while. Sadie had gone right back to work after the funeral, and her music had been a balm to her grief, but it had been selfish of her to only take care of herself. The repercussions hadn't been immediately evident, but she had let her mom down nine months ago, that was clear from her mother's current condition. Now she was home and she could make it up to her. She would make it better. Sadie patted her mom's leg through the bedcovers and left the room, shutting the door behind her, desperate to hide her emotions. She didn't want her mom to worry about her on top of the grief. That would make things worse.

Back down in the living room she sat at her drum set. She tapped out an even "thump, thump, thump" to match her guilty heartbeat. Picking up the sticks, she filled in the beat, humming the melody she had been working on. Turning the lyrics over in her head.

All of the lies you said
Tried to mess with my head.
I followed where you led
And now I'm left seeing red.

No more, no more. No more
No more, no more. No more

Promises you can't keep
The price I pay, way too steep
Boy you're in so, so deep
And honestly I can't sleep.

No more, no more. No more
No more, no more. No more

You say that you will but you never do it.
Your talk is cheap, yeah, I see right through it.

No coulds, shoulds or woulds gonna get you the goods
No more. No more.

Claiming it's love you make
Bending me 'til I break
My twisted and sad mistake
And I've had all that I can take.

No more, no more. No more
No more, no more. No more

You say that you're sorry but it doesn't matter
If I was queen I'd have your head on a platter.
No ifs, ands or buts gonna get what you want
No more. No more.

She pounded out the pain at the loss of her dad. She pounded out the guilt of leaving her mother behind while she returned to her career. And for good measure, she pounded out the anger at herself that she still carried around for putting up with Corey for too long.

Sadie was so caught up in the song she hadn't noticed her mother had come downstairs to join her until she heard the rhythmic strum of the guitar. As Sadie sang through the chorus again, her mom added a chord progression that filled out the sound.

Again as always, music was her therapy, and as she hummed the last of the tune and drummed out the closing measure with her mom harmonizing, a sense of peace filled her heart. She felt like the trite inspirational message on the side of a card store coffee mug: *Today is the first day of the rest of your life.*

*This was her fresh start.*

# CHAPTER FIVE

"No, no more!" Marley belted out the last line of the song.

Sadie gave the large tom two final smacks in time with Sophie's bass notes. "Whoo!" She celebrated, smiling at the rest of the group.

It was the first time their group had gotten together, and they had spent the past half hour working on the original song Sadie had written for them. Much to Sadie's astonishment, the women were actually starting to come together as a band, and everyone, including her mother strumming away on her guitar, seemed to be having a good time. By the time they ran through the song for the last time, everyone looked surprised and pleased with themselves.

Marley had been an absolute star all morning. First she had offered to host the coffee hour practice, then she had kept spirits buoyed as the ladies rumbled through their early attempts at making music together with her endless enthusiasm. Sadie had watched her closely as she kept an encouraging smile on her face, despite the wrong notes and bumbled lyrics that happened along the way. Marley had a way of keeping things chugging along even when the others' confidences faltered. It was an admirable quality. Sadie didn't know how she would repay her for jumping on board with the project so completely, but she would find a way.

"We sound like a real band." Kristen grinned and played a trill at the high end of the keyboard. "Now all we need is a name."

"Oh!" Marley's face lit up. "Some kind of nod to pop culture like Veruca Salt."

"Veruca Salt?" Sophie scrunched up her nose and shook her head, a mixture of distaste and confusion. "I don't know what that means."

"Veruca Salt was that spoiled rotten girl from *Willy Wonka and the Chocolate Factory*," Marley explained. "And then it was the name of a band in the nineties."

"We don't want to be named after some nasty little girl," Sophie argued.

"I think it's more the idea of a cult classic character as the name of the band." Sadie twirled a drumstick between her fingers as she mulled over possibilities. "Maybe something like Napoleon Dynamite or Buffy Summers."

"I've got it!" Kristen piped up. She played a few regal chords on the keyboard as if announcing her idea. "Regina Phalange. You know, from the TV show *Friends*. It's the alias of one of the characters. It's quirky and hip, and you know, wink-winky."

"Regina Phalange." Sadie said the name out loud to test it out. It wasn't half bad. "I think that could work."

"Regina Phalange." Marley repeated into the microphone with a grin. Somehow hearing the name through the practice speakers made it seem much more official. "We've got our name. That seals it. I think we're ready for a gig!"

"Yes!" Sadie pumped a fist in the air.

"No." A stern voice came across the room.

Jess.

"Oh honey, we're just joking around." Marley clicked her mic off and turned to her daughter. "You know, having a little fun."

"I'm all for fun." Jess's frown indicated otherwise as she twisted her blond ponytail around her finger. Based on the wrinkled graphic T-shirt and tattered gym shorts she was wearing, the ladies had woken her from sleep with their music. "But let's not get crazy here. This band thing isn't something you need to take on the road."

Sadie bit her lip hard to keep from speaking out of turn. She couldn't reconcile this Jess with the same smiling, charming woman she'd met poolside just days before. This version looked stressed and grumpy, and sure, maybe their rock 'n' roll coffee group could have waited until a later hour to make noise, but it was Marley's house and she'd seemed fine with it.

Suddenly Marley was fixing her daughter with a serious stare that indicated she was anything but fine with her behavior. "That's enough, Jess." To the women in the band she gave an apologetic half smile followed by an eyeroll that was clearly meant to convey the message, "Kids. What are you gonna do?"

"I think we've done a great job here today, ladies." Sadie tried to smooth over the awkward vibe as everyone began to pack up. "We'll take the weekend off and get back to it on Monday. That way we'll have a few practices before the party and the debut of Regina Phalange."

It had been Marley's idea to play a few songs at the party she was hosting for the neighborhood as a way to give the band something to work toward. Sadie was excited to perform in front of people again, and she had been on board as soon as it was mentioned. They had had to do a little work to convince the other women to go along with it, but since Marley pointed out it would be a good way to show the fun side of the cul-de-sac moms, they eventually came around.

Jess had busied herself hooking up a game system to the big screen television, and as the other women filed back up the stairs, Sadie stayed behind the drum set and waited until Jess acknowledged her sitting there.

"I assume this was your brilliant idea, rock star." Jess came behind the leather sofa to face Sadie. What had sounded like a term of endearment previously, now had a scarlet letter tone, like she was marking Sadie as bad news. Her face was hard, her features twisted into a snarl. She was clearly displeased with the whole band idea.

"What crawled up your ass, Moran?" Sadie scowled right back at her. "What the hell do you care how the neighborhood ladies spend their mornings?"

She crossed her arms and shrugged. "I don't care how everyone else spends their time, but what my mom does *is totally* my business."

"Um, she's an adult. I think she's capable of making her own decisions. She runs a business for God's sake." Sadie stood, hands on hips, ready to tell her where she could shove her controlling ways, but she stopped short, surprised by the television set lighting up behind Jess. Instead of the slick, modern graphics she had expected to pop up, the screen blinked and blipped alive with what appeared to be a menu of retro video games. Authentic eighties titles like Space Invaders, Centipede and Asteroid. Sadie had to remind herself she'd had enough of Jess Moran for one morning and tried not to look too impressed. Although, she kind of *did* have a hankering to play some Pitfall.

Jess's sharp voice brought Sadie's attention back to her. "Yes, she has her own business. All the more reason not to run around like she thinks she's some kind of pop princess teenager."

*Pop princess teenager?* That was what she saw happening that morning with the ladies making music in the basement?

"Okay." Sadie stuck her drumsticks in the back pocket of her cutoff jeans and sauntered past Jess toward the staircase. The band had made it through a great first rehearsal and she was not about to let Jess's bad mood and low-blow insults bring her down. "I'm gonna walk away before I say something I might regret, or, you know, throat punch you."

Sadie could have sworn Jess's mouth curved up in the tiniest bit of an amused smirk. "You got it, rock star."

When she reached the top of the stairs, still muttering under her breath about what a jerk Jess had been, she found Marley in the kitchen, staring down at her phone and looking displeased.

"What's wrong?" Sadie put a gentle hand on her shoulder, her musings about Jess's dark mood forgotten for the moment.

"Oh." Marley shook her head, clearly exasperated. She looked like she could use a hug, but Sadie didn't want to overstep. "Work problems. I have a new Queen of Hearts vodka flavor launch party scheduled tonight, and my assistant, Shanna, who usually emcees with Jess, has come down with some funky stomach bug and can't do it."

"So you're stuck filling in?" Sadie nodded sagely. Nothing like a last-minute work thing to bring you down.

"No, not me. I can't do that," Marley said simply.

Sadie waited for her to expand on the thought, but Marley's tight-lipped grimace indicated she wasn't going to offer anything further on the subject. Marley was usually a talker, no matter what the topic. It wasn't like her to clam up. Plus, it was weird—Marley didn't seem to mind fronting their band, but she wouldn't front her product? "Do you have another assistant you can call?"

"Only Jess and she's already going. There's no one else I can get to do it on such short notice. She'll have to do it alone, I guess." Marley sighed. "Unless…." She faced Sadie and placed both her hands squarely on her shoulders, looking her up and down while nodding approvingly. It was as if she was considering…

"Marley, no."

"Please, Sadie? It will be fun. It's like hosting a party."

If it was so much fun, why didn't Marley want to do it herself? Maybe it was some kind of business thing Sadie didn't get. The last thing Sadie wanted was to spend her Friday night with the grump bag she had left down in the basement, but she had the night off from Lenny's Pizza and she would probably be crashed out on the couch watching reruns on TV or playing video games anyway. And Marley had been so kind to her mom and so sweet to go along with the whole Regina Phalange thing. Sadie owed her one. She threw her hands up in surrender. "Okay. I'll do it."

"Yay!" Marley clapped her hands together. At least Sadie had made her happy. "I'm going to run upstairs and get you a Queen of Hearts shirt to wear. You own a black skirt, right?"

"Yep. I've got that covered."

"And wear heels, okay? We're going for sex appeal," she called over her shoulder as she hurried down the hallway.

Sadie groaned. Heels and sex appeal. Great. Plus the added bonus of hanging out with moody, broody Jess on her Friday night off from Lenny's. *Fun my ass.* But she would do it for Marley.

# CHAPTER SIX

Jess groaned as her pixelated green Frogger hopped one jump too far to the left and was met by a blocky eighteen-wheeler speeding down the highway. The taunting theme music played and GAME OVER flashed on the screen. She flung the controller onto the couch next to her and sank into the cushions. Her mind hadn't really been in the game. She had been too preoccupied replaying the scene with Sadie in her head—complete with Sadie marching angrily up the stairs.

There was one variation where she switched up the scene in her mind and instead of ending with both girls in a pissed-off huff, it ended with a tickle fight on the couch. A tickle fight that led to Jess tumbling on top of Sadie and pinning her down for a long, deep, earthshaking kiss.

*Okay, that kind of thinking had to stop.* There had to be some kind of happy medium. It was as if in her effort to shut down her flirt mode, she'd turned off her good graces altogether. She had acted like a total jerk in front of Sadie.

She hadn't been in the best mood to begin with since her morning had begun with a make-believe rock band, comprised of middle-aged moms practicing in the basement. But once those women started talking about taking the show on the road, her mood nosedived from bad to worse. Sadie, as the ringleader of this grand scheme, had been an easy target for Jess's ire.

Not that Sadie hadn't seemed more than capable of being on the receiving end of that ire. Had she actually threatened Jess with a *throat punch*? Jess grinned as she remembered the way Sadie had spit those words at her. Damn, that woman was sexy when she was angry. The way her eyes narrowed and jaw clenched, making those cute muscles in her cheek twitch. Not to mention her unwavering feistiness and sheer ability to stand up for herself and what she believed in. Having a strong will was hot as fuck on a woman. Jess wasn't a fan of wishy-washy girls who went along with the crowd. It wasn't how she was raised. But when Sadie stood there, hands on hips, hackles raised, poised for battle, it was all Jess could do to keep from taking her in her arms and kissing that smartass throat punch comment right off her sexy mouth.

Was Sadie equally as feisty in bed? Maybe she was one of those, "tough out in the real world, but submissive in the sack" types. Jess wouldn't mind finding out for herself. A flutter rose in her belly at the image of Sadie tangled up in her bedsheets.

"Jessica Rose Moran." Her mother's voice echoed down from the kitchen one floor above. Could she sense Jess was thinking about Sadie in a definite *not just friends* way? "Get up here, pronto."

Full name summons and 'pronto' in practically the same breath. Sounded serious. Jess and her mom had a different kind of relationship than a lot of her friends had with their mothers. They were a lot more Lorelei and Rory than most, but she had a level of respect for her mom, and when her full name was employed, she jumped to attention.

She clicked off the game system and bounded up the basement steps. As expected, her mom was waiting in the kitchen with a familiar, hands on hips stance, but with an uncharacteristic frown on her face.

"In what world do you think your behavior down there even remotely resembled being a friend to that girl?"

Jess's jaw dropped as her mind made sense of her mom's accusation. Had she been able to detect her tickle fight fantasy about Sadie? "My…behavior?"

"Yes, Jess. You came rumbling downstairs like a storm cloud settling over our coffee club and acted like the grumpiest grump to ever grump. You embarrassed me in front of my friends. And it was certainly no way to be a friend to Sadie DuChamp."

Her mom sure had a way with words, but still her point was made. When she needed to be full-on mom, Marley Moran had always been the no-nonsense type. She didn't hesitate to call Jess out on bullshit when deserved. She had certainly hit the mark this time.

Jess winced at the scolding, but there was more to her displeasure with the early morning band practice than a noise complaint, and they both knew it. Her ears burned as she choked back the emotion building in her. "Mom, it's great that you're all having so much fun, but they were talking about playing gigs in public. You can't get up and sing in front of people and draw that kind of attention to yourself."

"It's a backyard barbeque, hardly even public. Neighbors and friends who have seen me a million times. You're making a big deal out of nothing."

Jess shook her head. Her mom was dismissing it, but she had a valid concern. "It didn't sound like nothing when the other women were talking this morning. It sounded like a step one leading to an even bigger step two. And then what? It's not a good idea, and I don't like it. I worry about you, you know?"

"Oh, baby, I know you do." Her mom's posture relaxed and she pulled her daughter to her. "We're fooling around, helping out a friend. We're going to play at the neighborhood party for fun. Nobody is going to think any different of me for it. Besides, it's not like you're going to post it on social media. No one will even know except for the neighbors."

Jess surrendered to her mother's embrace. She rested her chin on her mom's shoulder and blew at the strands of blond hair that tickled her nose. They both had long hair nearly the same golden shade, only Jess's was natural and Marley's was not.

They both also had the same strong will. She was not going to win this battle. "Okay, Mom. Play at the party." She surrendered with a sigh. "Have fun. I just think you should be focusing all this energy on Queen of Hearts and our summer campaign."

"That reminds me." Her mom pulled out of the hug and held Jess at arm's length, her eyes suddenly wide and sparkling with the slightest hint of mischief. "Shanna bailed on the event tonight. I don't know what's gotten into her lately. She said she has a bug, but I have a weird feeling she was lying to me." She wrinkled up her nose like someone lying to her was on par with a bad smell. "But the good news is, I got Sadie to fill in for her. So you will have a second chance at this whole *be her friend* thing."

Right. More like working all evening with Sadie while trying her best not to flirt with her. Or worse, ending up acting like a total jerk in front of her again. This was not good news. "Wait. Are you sure Shanna is too sick to go? I mean, maybe she'll recover in time."

"I don't know." She shrugged. "She said she was sick. I was lucky to get Sadie on such short notice. So I will remind you once more: be on your best behavior. Be nice to the girl, okay?"

"I will, Mom. Promise." But she knew even as she said the words that it wasn't being nice that would be the problem.

# CHAPTER SEVEN

Sadie was waiting at the front door when Jess pulled up in Marley's white Lexus SUV. She smoothed her skirt and called up the stairs to her mom to let her know she was leaving, then carefully navigated down the front steps to the walk. She wasn't used to wearing high heels, and she would be damned if she was going to stumble or fall in front of Jess.

Sadie still hadn't reconciled the difference between "poolside Jess" and "early morning band practice Jess." She wasn't entirely sure she was ready to face either one of them again, but she had promised Marley she would work the event and that was what she would do. If she had to suffer through one night of awkwardness, so be it. She owed it to Marley. She would follow Jess's lead and roll with it. Sadie had repeated that mantra over and over as she curled her hair and perfected her smoky eye makeup. Her heartbeat sped up a notch as Jess hopped out of the driver's side of the car. She had a definite *go time* feeling.

Jess waved looking very neat and professional in her own short black skirt and maroon tank top with the Queen of Hearts logo embroidered on it. "Hey." She nodded, but her expression wasn't exactly warm. At least she was being polite, unlike earlier in the day.

"You brought your mom's car?" Sadie climbed in and waited for Jess's obvious answer to her stupid question while she ducked back into the driver's seat.

"Yes. Too many boxes to cram in the back of my Jeep." She pulled away from the curb and turned the volume on the radio up. Too damn stubborn to even make polite conversation, apparently.

Sadie shifted in her seat and tugged at the hem of her short skirt. She was still a little unsure about her duties for the event, and she was really hoping this silent treatment wasn't indicative of how the night would go. Sure, that morning Sadie had threatened to throat punch Jess, but she had totally had it coming then.

Plus, it wasn't as if she was going to do that to her while they were running Marley's event. Maybe she had managed to put a little fear into Jess and that was why she was so silent. "Are you scared of me?" Sadie pushed the issue, squinting and giving her a sideways glance.

That big, sexy smile slid across Jess's face, but she kept her eyes glued to the road in front of them. "Not a chance. Nice try, though, rock star."

"Then what's with the awkward silence?"

"Awkward to you, maybe." She shrugged. "I'm trying to collect my thoughts for the job. Get mentally prepared."

Sadie reached forward and turned down the radio. "While blasting *Panic! At The Disco?* Not exactly the soundtrack to meditation."

"Hey, it gets me in the zone."

"Well I need you to talk to me to get me in the zone. I'm still not really sure about what's going on here tonight." Unsure was a lie. She was downright nervous. Marley had said her main duties were to look good and act like a party host. To make sure people were sampling the vodkas, especially the new flavors they were launching at the event, Upside-Down Pineapple Cake and

Swedish Fish, and to make sure the guests were having a good time in general. "What specifically are we going to be doing?"

"You and I are like the Masters of Ceremony for this event," Jess explained with a patient tone that was strikingly different from her mood earlier in the day. "Bartenders will be serving Queen of Hearts vodka drinks and cocktail waitresses will be handing out samples of the two new flavors. There will be a deejay who'll get people up and dancing. We'll mingle with the crowd, and at some point we will hand out the T-shirts I had printed up with our logo."

"So, our job is to party and give people stuff?" Sadie dumbed it down to a single sentence.

"Yep." Jess kept her hands on the wheel but shrugged her shoulders.

"That sounds like a great job."

Jess laughed and finally glanced over to make eye contact. Sadie's insides betrayed her and went all gooey at stubborn Jess's lopsided grin. Sadie still hadn't forgiven her for that "pop princess" comment from earlier that morning, no matter what her traitorous, hardening nipples seemed to think.

"It can be fun," Jess assured her. "Turn on the ol' charm, okay? You must have some in there somewhere, rock star. And under no circumstances are you to threaten to throat punch anybody."

So she hadn't forgotten either. "Oh, I save those kinds of moves for the really special people, don't worry."

"Aw, you think I'm *special*." Jess drew out the last word in an annoying sing-song tone.

"I think you're lucky I didn't follow through with the threat."

Jess was still smiling when they reached the parking lot of the club where they were holding the event. She pulled the Jeep up to the entrance so they could unload the T-shirts. They dragged out three large boxes of Queen of Hearts swag, but when Sadie reached for a smaller one tucked behind them, Jess waved her off. "We don't need that one. These three will do it."

Sadie stood on the curb with the boxes, while Jess parked and then hustled back. She waited, glancing down at her outfit—a mirror image of the one Jess was wearing. The maroon shirt with "Queen of Hearts" embroidered in sparkly silver lettering fit tight and sexy. She would have to make a conscious effort not to repeatedly tug down her black skirt all night. And of course there were the black heels that were an ankle sprain hazard. They were two women dressed to pimp some vodka.

Jess briefed her as they walked through the main part of the club to the back deck overlooking the lake. A few patrons sat at the bar dividing the indoor section from the outdoor area where the deejay was already setting up and staff was bustling around stocking barware and bottles of vodka. "The crowd is made up of owners of local establishments where we are hoping to sell the product, and of course their guests. Some of the old guys can be a little crass when they get a little liquor in them, but try to take it with a grain of salt. They're full of hot air, but they're still clients."

Jess was carrying two of the boxes, and Sadie couldn't help but notice the way her arm muscles flexed, straining the fabric of her top. Meanwhile, Sadie struggled to get her one box through the club without dropping it. It wasn't heavy, but it was awkward to carry, especially in heels. *Must look cool and pimp vodka.*

"Are you listening to me?" Jess glanced over her shoulder.

"Yes. Hot air-filled clients. Got it," she repeated dutifully.

"Right," she continued. "But that being said, they have no right to take things too far. If anyone makes you uncomfortable, *anyone*, let me know. The bouncers here don't fuck around and they know me. They'll take care of it."

Sadie couldn't help herself. "I could just—"

"No throat punches." Jess cut her off as they reached the tables that served as the final destination for the T-shirts. She dropped her boxes to the floor and rubbed her lower back as she straightened up again. "Okay, we'll get this stuff set up, and then we'll…" Her voice trailed off as if she had lost her train of thought.

Sadie followed her gaze over to the bar to a skinny brunette hunched over with her head cradled in her candy apple red manicured hands. A pretty woman. Of course. That would be the thing that would make Jess drop everything. "Earth to Jess. Hello?"

"Yeah. Um. Give me a minute, okay?" She strode over to the woman leaving Sadie to stand alone awkwardly staring after her.

"Sure. I'll wait here while you go hit on some beautiful woman at the bar." Sadie said to Jess's back, but her voice was lost in the music and din of party prep in the club. She eyed the abandoned boxes of promotional swag and tapped her high-heeled foot impatiently. Was she supposed to unload the Queen of Hearts stuff while Jess got her flirt on? No. Hell no. That was not how the night was going to go down. Blood pounded in her ears and she blew out a big breath. She had to put an end to this crap or she would spend the whole night working while Jess prowled the club for ladies.

Throwing her shoulders back, she marched herself right over to Jess ready to give her an earful about her work ethic, but as she got closer, Sadie realized the brunette in her happy, floral-print sundress was crying. Was Jess hitting on some sad girl? Taking advantage of a woman who was down? That was low. That was a whole new level of crappiness from Jess.

She tapped Jess on the shoulder none too gently, not caring one bit that she was interrupting the women. "Were you seriously going to leave me over there while you—"

"Thanks, Sadie. I could use a hand here." Jess kept one hand on the woman's back as she spoke over her shoulder. "We need to get something in this girl's stomach. Bread or crackers—something to absorb the alcohol. Poor thing's had a little too much fun with her friends."

"Some friends. They left me here!" The poor thing slurred and wiped the back of her hand across her teary eyes.

The beautiful brunette was trashed. Jess wasn't trying to pick her up; she was trying to help. Sadie couldn't quite form words as she realized her error. She had totally misread the situation and misjudged Jess.

"Can you go over there and grab a couple packets of saltines?" Jess continued as she tipped her head in the direction of the servers' station. "Tell the servers you're with Queen of

Hearts. They won't mind. I'm going to order her some coffee. We'll try to sober her up and then call her an Uber."

Sadie nodded and followed orders to retrieve the crackers, her cheeks hot with embarrassment at her snap judgment. Jess wasn't pulling some shady move. She was trying to help someone in need of a friend. Basing her expectations for Jess's behavior on one bad mood had been unfair. Everybody was entitled to a bad morning now and again. She silently vowed to do better by Jess and give her a clean slate as far as first impressions went. By the time she returned to the bar, Jess had pried the bottle of beer out of the woman's hand and replaced it with a tall glass of water.

"Is she okay? Did you order the Uber?" Sadie shouted above the deejay's music as she deposited the packets of crackers on the bar.

Jess immediately tore into one and offered it to her new friend. "A car should be here in five minutes. As long as she gets a little food in her stomach, I think Allie here is going to be fine. But I'm going to wait with her until her ride arrives."

Sadie nodded, still feeling a bit sheepish about her assumption about Jess's motives for approaching Allie in the first place. "Do you want some help getting her out front?"

Jess smiled gratefully and gave Sadie's shoulder a squeeze. "Thanks, rock star."

The tension that had built in Sadie's shoulders receded as a smile formed on her lips. Jess's nickname for her was starting to gain back a certain charm.

Once Allie had left, they got right back to business. Together they emptied the boxes, setting the contents neatly on the maroon cloth-covered tables, making piles of the key fobs, beaded necklaces, plastic shot glasses, and T-shirts they would hand out over the course of the night. After that Jess introduced Sadie to the servers who would be helping with the drink samples. The waitstaff consisted of leggy model types who seemed to stride around with much more confidence than Sadie had in high heels. The way they zipped around the bar left her feeling as ungraceful as a flamingo on roller skates. Jess, on the other hand, was the picture of professionalism as she spoke to them, giving instructions for the evening.

The deejay kept the music spinning and the crowd trickled in. There had to be over a hundred partiers at the peak. Sadie made conversation with several of the guests, always careful to loop it back to Queen of Hearts in one way or another. She even made an appearance on the dance floor shaking her booty along with a group of women who had all come representing a local tavern. She had fun while she worked, but the highlight of the event for her was when it was time for her and Jess to step up onto the makeshift stage with the deejay and thank everyone for their support of the Queen of Hearts vodka.

Jess did all the talking, but Sadie was right by her side, beaming her biggest, brightest smile to those in attendance. Being an ambassador for the company felt a lot like being a celebrity. All eyes were on them as Jess delivered her speech, impressing Sadie with her public speaking capabilities. She was much more articulate than she had been earlier that morning when she was groaning and grunting at the band practice. At the end of the spiel, when the crowd busted out in hoots and applause, Jess grabbed Sadie's hand in hers and raised them up above their heads in a kind of victory pose. A jolt of adrenaline shot through Sadie, tingling its way up her spine and into her head, giving her a rush. It was similar to the way she felt on stage when she was playing drums—power swirling in her stomach and pulsing through her veins. A total high.

From there the night went smoothly as the party wound down, and they continued to mingle with the guests. The new flavors had been well received, everyone was having a good time with their vodka drinks, and before Sadie knew it, the deejay was announcing "last call."

Sadie was organizing the leftover shirts when she spotted one of the servers, Audrey, out on the pier, looking less than thrilled with one of the guests. She recognized him as Grant, the owner of a small bar in the same neighborhood as Lenny's Pizza. He looked to be in his late forties, with close-cropped hair that was graying at the temples. He was a big, barrel-chested guy in a sports jacket and jeans—the kind of guy who probably played football in high school, maybe even college, but then fell back on his business degree when his glory days came to an end. Even from a distance, Sadie could see something was off with the interaction. Thanks to her ex-boyfriend Corey, she was all too familiar with the look of a man who had consumed too much alcohol and had turned grabby and entitled. It was a tiny step away from mean drunk and could turn on a dime. She glanced over at Jess, hoping to get the okay to intervene and a little backup, but she was engrossed in a conversation with a client. Sadie waved to get her attention, but all she got in return was a nod, indicating Jess would be over in a minute.

Grant had a strong hold on Audrey's forearm, even though she tried to twist out of his grasp. Sadie's pulse throbbed in her temples as her heartbeat picked up. She couldn't stand by and watch a woman be treated that way—she had to help. She skittered as fast as her pointy, heeled footwear would take her across the deck and out onto the pier. "Hey, let her go!"

Audrey yanked her arm free as Grant turned his drunken scowl on Sadie, but then his expression shifted. The presence of another person on the pier seemed to be enough to snap him back to reality, and he'd realized how inappropriate his behavior was. A flicker of shock passed over his ruddy face before he closed his eyes and shook his head as if clearing it.

"I, uh, was trying to talk to her," he slurred as Audrey took a big step away from him.

As Sadie moved to step between them, the heel on her right shoe caught between the wooden planks beneath her, jolting her to a stop. As if she didn't look ridiculous enough tripping herself while on a rescue mission, it was made ten times worse because when Sadie stopped, she felt someone crash against her—Jess.

On the bright side, the impact freed Sadie's heel from between the boards. On the not-so-bright side, Jess's momentum pushed both of them right over the edge of the pier. Sadie kicked her legs like a cartoon character as the ground disappeared beneath them, and the din of the music from the dance floor dropped away as Jess cried out in slow motion, "Oh crap!" Then together they hit the surface of the dark, dank lake water.

The water wasn't very deep by the pier, and Sadie managed to keep her head above it, but the splash they had made upon impact soaked her hair and face anyway. Sputtering against the wetness, she glanced over to see how her counterpart had fared.

Jess seemed to have found her footing as she pushed her long, soggy blond hair out of her eyes. "At least the party is over." She shrugged and gave another of those lopsided grins that set Sadie's heart soaring, even while soaking wet in a gross lake.

They only eyed each other for a moment before both breaking out in a fit of laughter.

Sadie did her best to dry out using the hand dryers in the ladies' room of the club. She changed into a leftover, men's XL T-shirt that she knotted at her waist, then ventured back out to the deck. The majority of the guests and servers had cleared out and the deejay had packed it in for the night, leaving just a few late-night drinkers at the bar. She found Jess, also in a fresh shirt, packing things up.

"Well, that was a party we won't soon forget," Sadie said with a smirk as she sidled up to Jess who was tucking a few last items into a cardboard box. She couldn't get over the difference between this professional, commanding Jess and the one who was brooding and grumpy only hours before at the house. She much preferred this version.

"You know what they say. It's not a party until someone falls in the lake."

"Nobody says that." Sadie shook her head but laughed in spite of herself.

Jess raised her eyebrows and said in a teasing tone, "They might after tonight, though."

"What's your mom going to think? I totally made a scene at her event."

"She's probably going to get a pretty good laugh out of it. And then maybe give you a lesson in walking in those things." She nodded at Sadie's pointy-toed shoes.

Sadie had been surprised at the grace and poise Jess had demonstrated all evening in her own high heels. She had expected the athletic woman to be out of her element in heels, but Jess had proved her totally wrong, still going strong even though it was after two a.m.

Sadie balled up fists on her hips defensively. "I can walk in these things just fine, thank you very much. The heel got jammed between the boards. It could have happened to anyone."

"Yet it only happened to you, rock star."

She shot Sadie a withering look before relaxing into a big grin that reached her eyes, causing a distinct flutter in Sadie's core.

"Come on, let's get out of here," Jess said.

The leftover supplies fit into one box that Jess hitched up on her hip and carried back to the car. She took the keys from Jess's hand and unlocked and lifted the tailgate for her. "Oh, what about that other box?" The smaller container was still tucked in the back of the cargo space.

"Actually, you should grab that. It's for you."

"You had Queen of Hearts shirts made for me?" Sadie pulled it toward her as instructed.

Jess slid the larger box in the back of the car and crossed her arms. "Not exactly. Go ahead. Open it."

She couldn't read the expression on Jess's face—brows pushed together, gaze locked on Sadie's, the grin from earlier was gone. Sadie peeled the packing tape from the seam and lifted the cardboard flaps. And then she gasped.

It contained T-shirts, but not for Queen of Hearts. Sadie pulled out the one on top and gave it a shake to get a good look. It was a black cotton ladies' cut T-shirt with a white screen print of a "Hello, my name is" badge with REGINA PHALANGE filled in as the name.

"There are enough for the whole band." A smile played at Jess's lips, clearly pleased with Sadie's stunned reaction.

"You made us T-shirts?"

"Yes, I did." She nodded, and her expression shifted to a more solemn one. "I was a total jerk to you and the other ladies this morning and I want to apologize. I'm glad that you and Mom's friends are having fun with your music, and I'm really sorry for putting that down. Truth is, you did sound really good."

Sadie searched her face waiting for there to be a punchline, afraid that this was all a big joke. But she found nothing but sincerity in Jess's clear blue-green eyes. Her jaw twitched, and Sadie realized she was waiting for a response.

Jess had made something to show her support for the band. She didn't just say she was sorry. But she *showed* it. Sadie's body flushed warm, and before she could overthink it, she threw her arms around Jess in a tight hug. "Thank you, Jess. That was so sweet of you."

She meant it too. With all the disappointments she'd had with relationships in the past few months—breaking up with Corey and Sugar Stix falling apart—it felt reassuring to know there were people who took responsibility for their actions. People who cared about others and actually bothered to make things right.

The muscles in Jess's strong shoulders rippled beneath Sadie's arms. Resting her chin against Jess's neck, Sadie inhaled her citrusy scent. A tingle slid down her spine, bringing her back to her senses. She quickly released Jess from her grasp and her cheeks went hot, embarrassed that she had flung herself at someone she hardly knew.

"I...uh...I really like the shirts, Jess. Thank you," she stammered. To her relief, Jess continued to smile and didn't look at all put off by her emotional reaction.

"You're welcome. Now, come on. Let's get home and get this eau de lake off." She gestured at her soggy hair. By the time Sadie was settled in her seat, Jess hopped into the driver's side and started the car. "I gotta admit, naming your band Regina Phalange was a total lesbian power move. Big props for that."

"Lesbian power move?" Sadie eyed Jess trying to sort out what she meant. "It's a *Friends* reference. You know, the television show?"

"No, I'm familiar with the show and the reference." Jess kept her gaze firmly on the road, her face emotionless to keep Sadie guessing if she was kidding or serious. "But Regina Phalange translates to 'Finger Queen' in Latin and you can't get much more lesbian than the Finger Queen, rock star." She shrugged to indicate it was simply a matter of fact. "Was that some kind of joke about someone's sexuality?"

*Finger Queen?* That wasn't what the band's name was about at all. She certainly hadn't meant it as a joke about Jess being a lesbian. Sadie's scalp prickled with embarrassment as she shook her head. After all the ground they had gained that night, she didn't want to offend Jess now. "The name has nothing to do with my sexuality or anyone else's." Her brain grasped for some kind of proof to present on her behalf. "Regina Phalange wasn't even my idea. It was Kristen's. It really was—"

"Sadie." Jess grinned before reaching across the console and fist bumping her thigh. "I'm totally messing with you."

Relief washed over Sadie as she blew out her breath and slumped back in her seat. Crisis averted. "You are a real piece of work, you know that?"

"I like to keep you on your toes, rock star," Jess laughed.

"Don't worry, you do a damn good job of it."

In spite of the teasing, Sadie's brain still struggled to fight off the image it had conjured up minutes earlier at Jess's suggestion of showering up...those shoulder muscles glimmering under droplets of water, especially after Jess suggesting the title of Finger Queen for one of them. Jess was right. It was sexual when put in that context. Sadie couldn't think about Jess in that way. She *could*, but she shouldn't. This was a woman who called her "rock star" ironically, a woman who had been miserable to her that morning. She had to rein the conversation in. She stared out the side window into the darkness. "Do you know why I started the band?"

"Why?"

"I'm hoping it will bring a little joy back into my mom's life. Give her something to focus on, you know?" She kept her gaze fixed on the blur of streetlights they passed. She felt braver that way. "I think she's been really lonely since my dad died. I was in New York and she was all alone. That's why I'm gonna stick around a while now. To make sure she's okay."

A beat of silence passed before Jess spoke. "I think that's really good of you. I'm sure your mom appreciates it. And Regina Phalange is a fine name for a band."

A snort of laughter escaped Sadie before she could stop it. "We are blessed to have your approval," she said dryly and finally dared to look at Jess again. It felt good to confide in her about her mom. *Really good.*

She swallowed hard and took a deep breath to compose herself. She was in town to help her mom sort things out. The last thing she needed was to fall for the first person in Tucker Pointe who showed her a little kindness. She wasn't some weak-minded girl. Never was, never would be. The last time she had let down her guard—when she was dating Corey—it had led to nothing good. She had learned that lesson the hard way.

So why couldn't she stop wondering if she should picture tan, taut abs on Jess in that shower fantasy?

Jess parked her mother's SUV in the driveway and followed the stone path around the back of the house and past the pool. She entered through the back door directly into the kitchen like she usually did. It was late, but she suspected Mom had waited up for her. Based on the distant hum of the late-night reruns coming from the television in the den, she was correct.

"Mom, are you awake?" She peered into the dimly lit room where her mom was stirring, but draped across the couch as if perhaps she had dozed off while waiting.

"Yes, baby, come in and tell me about the night. It looks like you had a long one. What happened to you?" Her mom sat up and dragged her afghan across the couch to make room for Jess to join her.

"I took a dip in the lake. It's a long story." Jess plopped down on the overstuffed cushion and gestured at the police procedural crime drama on the television. Her mother had seen every episode of the series at least once. "I don't know why you watch this stuff, especially late at night. All the psychopaths and murderers on that show, doesn't it give you nightmares after…" she caught herself before she said too much. It was late. No need to upset her mom. "You know."

Her mom reached for the remote and clicked the television off. "Some of the episodes are a bit disturbing, but in the end the good guys always come out on top. That's why I watch, I think. I like to know there are people out there fighting for what's right. Keeping the rest of us safe."

Jess smiled at her mother all snuggled up on the couch in her jersey cotton pajamas and her heart filled with love. After everything life had thrown at her, her mom was still positive and hopeful. It was one of the many qualities her mother possessed that she admired.

"So, come on." Her mom squeezed her knee. "Tell me about your night."

Jess could've told her how she couldn't keep her eyes off Sadie in that little black skirt. Or how the way Sadie bit her bottom lip when she was nervous gave her a tingle in her middle. Instead she stuck to the basics. "It went fine. Sadie did a great job and I think we worked well together."

"Good." Mom's smile hinted that she might be a little too happy about Jess and Sadie working well together, but Jess ignored it.

"And I brought you this." Jess handed Mom the Regina Phalange T-shirt she'd brought in with her.

She held up the black cotton shirt in front of her and her face lit up with a bright smile when she realized what it was. "You made this for me? Oh, baby, thank you." She grabbed Jess's arm and pulled her into a hug despite the lingering scent of lake that clung to her.

"I made one for each of the ladies in Regina Phalange." Jess's voice was muffled by her mouth pressing against her mother's shoulder as she confessed, "And one for me too."

"That was very sweet." Her mom kissed the top of her head before finally releasing her from her embrace. "I know you're not wild about the band playing at the party, but it's a one-off. Practicing has been a great excuse to get Jennifer out of the house on a regular basis and the performance is a goal for us to work toward. Actually, I think the ladies are all having a good time with it. I know I am."

"Mom, if you don't think this is too risky, I'm going to trust you." Jess stood and stretched. A big yawn escaped her. Her mother's nonchalance at putting herself in the spotlight wasn't exactly reassuring, but it had been a long day and she still needed to get in the shower and wash off the last of the lake slime. Her quick bar towel bath in the club restroom didn't quite cut it. This battle could be fought at another time. "I think I'm going to call it a night."

"Sounds good." Her mom blew her a kiss from her cozy spot on the couch. "I'll probably be right behind you."

Jess kicked her heels off before taking the steps two at a time up to her room. As she peeled off her Queen of Hearts tank top, she grinned, recalling Sadie's expression when she asked about the origin of Regina Phalange's name. She couldn't help herself. She had to test the waters to see if Sadie flinched at the word *lesbian*. Happily, Sadie had passed the test with flying colors, if not with reddened cheeks.

Jess had been touched by the way Sadie protected the server who had been cornered by the drunk dude at the club. Sadie hadn't hesitated to step in and stand up for the other woman—a commendable quality in Jess's eyes. Even if it had resulted in the two of them taking a dunk in the lake. Heat flooded Jess's core as she remembered Sadie resurfacing in that wet shirt. There was no denying Sadie was a beautiful girl.

Catching a glimpse of herself in the mirror, she noticed the silly grin on her face while she reminisced about the night. *Oh no. No, no, no.* The night had been fun, and Sadie had proven herself to be more than just a rock 'n' roll gal, but Jess couldn't let herself get carried away. Sadie was not some girl she could pull the ol' "Date and Dash" on like the others who came and went from her life. She and Sadie's moms were friends and they were neighbors. There would be no avoiding the girl if things went south. No. It was best to repeat the mantra she had taken on when she had first met Sadie: just friends. That was it. Nothing more.

With that thought, she stepped into the bathroom to enjoy a nice, cold shower.

# CHAPTER EIGHT

When Sadie got home from working the lunch shift at Lenny's on Thursday afternoon, she found her mother dressed in jeans and a plaid button-down shirt vacuuming the living room, half-humming, half-singing one of the songs the band had been working on for the upcoming party at Marley's.

She balanced the pizza box she had brought home from work on her hip and grinned at the sight of her mom shaking her hips along to the beat of "Kiss Me Deadly." It had been a long time since she had seen her mom like this—impulsive, carefree, and dressed in normal clothes even though she wasn't leaving the house.

"Hi," she called out over the noise of the vacuum, waving her free hand to get her mother's attention. "What's going on here?"

Her mom shut off the machine and wiped the back of her hand across her forehead to chase away beads of sweat. Her cheeks were red as she adjusted the bandana that tied up her hair. "Oh, Sadie, I didn't hear you come in. I'm trying to clean up a bit."

"I meant the singing," Sadie teased as she set the veggie pie on the dining room table. Seeing the joy on her mother's face instantly energized her, despite the fact that she had been on her feet for the better part of the day. She wanted to keep the good feeling going—to share it with her mom. "I definitely heard some singing. 'Come on pretty baby, kiss me deadly!'" She belted out the last words to drive her point home.

"Was I singing?" She waved a dismissive hand as if she didn't know what her daughter was talking about, but she smiled as she followed Sadie across the room. "That song has been stuck in my head all day. Well, that one and the Regina Phalange original. 'You say that you're sorry but it doesn't matter. If I was queen I'd have your head on a platter. No ifs, ands or buts gonna get what you want.'"

"'No more. No more. No more!'" Sadie joined in on the chorus before the two of them dissolved into giggles.

Her mom put a hand to her belly and leaned the other on the kitchen table to keep her balance as she let her sillies out. Sadie couldn't remember the last time she heard her mother's laughter and it was music to her ears. Music had been the key to boosting her spirits like Sadie had hoped. The plan was working.

"Mom, maybe we should put you on the microphone? That was awesome." Sadie grinned.

"Oh, no. I'm doing fine singing in the background, thank you very much." She straightened her bandana again. "Besides, the awesomeness of that song is completely credited to you. I am so proud of you and your amazing songwriting skills. I knew you were making music all that time in New York, but I had no idea what you were really doing. I didn't know you had this amazing talent to write the way you do."

Sadie's heart swelled with pride. Between the compliments and the change in her mom's mood, she could practically float away on the joy she was feeling. "Thanks, Mom." Happy tears threatened and before they could fall, she changed the subject. She didn't want to risk ruining the mood by being overly emotional. "Come on, we should eat before this gets cold."

Her mom gestured at the pizza box on the table. "What did you bring home today?"

with experience. But I couldn't drag myself out of bed. Trying to sleep off another late night of schlepping vodka."

Truth was Jess had been awakened by the musical stylings of Regina Phalange and immediately regretted not planning ahead. The nine a.m. practice was already underway when she fully roused herself from slumber, and by the time she would have cleaned up enough to be presentable in front of Sadie after being out late at another Queen of Hearts event, she would have missed the whole thing anyway. She had lain in bed and listened from afar, biding her time until she could make a decent impression on the woman she was so eager to see again.

"Ah, too much partying." Sadie nodded knowingly and gave her a teasing wink. Jess had caught her in a cheerful mood. "But you don't have to apologize. It's not like you're in the band." Her mouth opened to a mock shocked O. "Wait a minute. Are you trying to say you would like to join Regina Phalange? Do you want to be in the band?"

Despite her lack of musical ability, joining the band was an actual thought that had crossed Jess's mind more than once since Regina Phalange's inception. Her last foray into the music world back in high school hadn't gone so great, but she was willing to give it another shot under the circumstances. If she was in the band she would have a reason to hang out with them, which accomplished two of her goals—keeping an eye on her mom's plans for this party performance and spending more time with Sadie. She covered up her ulterior motives with a snicker. "Me? Playing in the band? No. I tried that in high school and had zero success." She shook her head. "I enjoy music, but I cannot make music."

"Hm." Sadie sucked her bottom lip between her teeth and regarded Jess from head to toe, as if sizing her up for assignment. "You're strong and quick, and fun to have around—I mean, *most* of the time."

"Ha ha."

Sadie gave a firm nod indicating she had made up her mind. "I think you would make a damn good roadie."

A peal of laughter burst from Jess in spite of her efforts to hold it in. "A roadie? You want me to be a roadie for your band?"

"You said you can't make music, but it seems like you want to be involved." Sadie shrugged. "I was trying to include you. But if you aren't interested—"

"I'll do it. I'll be the roadie for Finger Queen."

From the way Sadie bit her lip again it appeared to be her turn to struggle to keep a straight face. "Say it right or I'll remove you from your position before you even get started."

Warmth flushed Jess's body at the decidedly flirty tone the conversation had suddenly taken. Everything sounded like a sex reference to her. "God, you've turned bossy. Who made you Finger Queen anyway?"

"Say it right." Sadie repeated her warning, but her eyes were bright with teasing.

Jess let out a defeated sigh and fixed her expression into what she hoped conveyed sincerity. "I want to be a roadie for Regina Phalange."

"We would love to have you on board." Sadie reached out her hand to shake on the deal.

Taking Sadie's hand in her own sent a spark of electricity right up her arm and into her body. "Then I guess that's that." She grinned and held onto Sadie a beat longer than necessary. Surprisingly, she didn't want the touch to end. She didn't want her time with Sadie to end at all. "Hey, we should celebrate. Wanna get a beer or something tonight?"

"That sounds nice, but I can't tonight." Sadie's smile faded slightly and she pulled her hand back to her side. "I'm doing something with my mom. Maybe another time, though?"

Disappointment washed over Jess. Had she read the signs all wrong? It had seemed like they were getting on okay, so maybe Sadie really did have plans with her mom. She stretched her arms above her head hoping to distract from the embarrassment burning in her cheeks. "Sure. Another time would be great too." She bounced on the balls of her feet, anxious to escape the sudden awkwardness. "I, uh, guess I better get back to my run."

The remainder of the smile left on Sadie's face dropped and her brows knitted together over her caramel-brown eyes. "Oh, okay. I'll see you later then?"

"You got it, rock star." Jess managed to flash a carefree grin and give a wink before she took off down the street.

As she picked up her pace, Jess churned the conversation over and over. It had seemed like a smooth transition to ask Sadie out for a drink. Had she imagined the flirty vibe between them? The offer could have been a "just friends" thing. It didn't have to be a date. Maybe Sadie had the good sense to shut it down before things went too far. Yes. It was better that way. Jess didn't need to start anything with the daughter of her mom's friend. One of them would probably end up getting hurt and then they would both feel bad.

When she reached the end of the road, she turned and headed back toward home. She could admit the abrupt ending to the conversation with Sadie had been for the best, but she couldn't deny that another nice, cold shower had worked its way up on her to-do list.

Sadie grabbed the junk mail out of the box and strode toward the house without a backward glance at Jess. She couldn't bear it after the breakneck turn the conversation had taken. She thought things had been going well between them, but then Jess had suddenly gone running off again. It was as if Jess couldn't stand getting too comfortable with Sadie before a switch flipped in her mind and she had to distance herself. She literally ran away.

Was it the way Sadie had declined Jess's offer for a beer? She hadn't meant to shoot her down. Hell, she didn't want to shut her down. Sadie shuffled the junk mail in her hands, unable to stop the grin spreading across her face as she imagined sitting in the dark corner of a bar having a quiet conversation with Jess. She wouldn't mind spending a little time getting to know her better, but for that night it was going to be Sadie and her mom. She had to take advantage of the good mood in their household while it lasted. Maybe if she kept her mother's mood going, everything would be okay again. First she had a good afternoon, and then they would have their fun movie night out. It was worth a try, even if it meant missing out on a beer with Jess this time.

"Mom, I have a great idea," she called out cheerfully as she entered the house. "Mom?"

Her mom was no longer standing at the dinner table where she had left her, and she wasn't responding to Sadie's voice. A closer look past the abandoned pizza box showed a portion of the previous stack of mail had been sorted—a stack of magazines and glossy catalogues, some torn envelopes that appeared to be discarded junk mail, and then a third pile of mail addressed to Jack DuChamp, Sadie's father.

Sadie's heart sunk. Her mother must have only gotten as far as sorting the mail before she was overwhelmed by her grief again. Sadie hurried up the steps but wasn't surprised when she found her mother's bedroom door closed.

She lightly rapped her knuckles on it. "Mom, are you in there? Are you okay?" When there was no response, she gently opened the door and poked her head in.

The blinds were pulled and her mother was tucked in bed. She stirred slightly at Sadie's presence. "Hey, baby. I think I overdid it a bit. I'm worn out."

Sadie wasn't ready to give up that easily. There had been a real change in her mom when she'd come home from work. There had to be some way to get that back. "How about you rest for a while and when you get up, we can go to the movies. Doesn't that sound fun?"

"It does sound fun, but I'm not up to it tonight, sweetie. I'm sorry. Close the door on your way out, okay?" She rolled over and pulled the covers up to her head, ending the conversation.

Sadie blew out a long breath as she closed the door behind her. She didn't get it. Her mom had been singing Regina Phalange songs earlier—smiling and even laughing. The music had made a difference, but now the spell was broken.

With a whole, empty evening laid out before her, Sadie headed back down the stairs to put the pizza away. Jess might still be available to hang out, but Sadie wasn't wild about leaving her mom home alone after the relapse in mood. Of course, that didn't mean Jess couldn't join her. She pulled out her phone and tapped out a text.

*If that offer for a beer tonight still stands, why don't you stop over here tonight?* Her phone beeped with a response before she even got the leftover pizza to the fridge.

*Sounds great. Lager okay?*

# CHAPTER NINE

Sadie inspected her reflection in the mirror and raked her fingers through her hair, pushing the loose waves into a rumpled style. A swipe of pink lip gloss was all she needed to finish her look. She capped the tube, then troubled the hoop in her eyebrow with her fingertips for good measure. There was no reason for her to feel nervous about Jess's arrival at the house. They'd hung out before, but this was the first time it was the two of them alone. She'd picked out her outfit of ripped denim shorts and a paisley print peasant blouse, and even given herself a little spritz of perfume, but they were only going to hang out at the house. She didn't need to be fancy. She was spending time with a friend from the neighborhood. Someone she had worked with. Their mothers were friends for heaven's sake.

Sadie hadn't even mentioned to her mother that she was expecting company that evening, although she hadn't actually had occasion to. Her mom had remained holed up in her bedroom for the rest of the afternoon once she'd retreated there. Sadie had tried to persuade her to come downstairs for dinner around seven o'clock, but in the end, she'd taken her a tray with a sandwich and a bowl of soup, and she'd eaten her own meal alone.

She twirled a beaded leather wrap bracelet around her wrist and fastened it in place as she headed out of her room. The doorbell rang announcing Jess's arrival.

In spite of her efforts to stay cool, Sadie couldn't help but break out in a smile when she opened the door to find Jess posed against the post of the front porch holding out a six-pack of longnecks. She invited her inside and led her down to the game room in the basement.

"Welcome to the party room at Chez DuChamp." Sadie spread her arms in a gesture of showcasing the area. "Please make yourself at home."

The girls circled the billiards table in the middle of the room as Jess appeared to take in her surroundings. The table was covered with clothes that were in the middle of being sorted much like the mail on the dining room table upstairs, but Jess pushed a stack of jeans out of the way and set the bottles of beer down. "Guess we're not playing pool tonight."

"Yeah." Heat rushed Sadie's cheeks and her scalp began to tingle with embarrassment. She had been so excited to show Jess her reason for bringing her down to the game room that she hadn't even thought about what the pool table looked like. As her brain stammered for a reasonable excuse, her mouth surprisingly spit out the truth. "My mom is still kinda mid-project. She's slowly sorting through my dad's stuff, but it's taking her a while. I'm letting her go at her own pace, you know?"

Jess's face blanched and her jaw dropped as she covered her open mouth with her hand. "Oh my god, Sadie. I'm so sorry. I really put my foot in it. I didn't mean—"

"It's okay."

Her blue eyes went even wider. "It's not okay," she insisted. "That was the most insensitive thing I could have said, and I sincerely apologize." Jess put a gentle hand on Sadie's shoulder and looked squarely at Sadie, regret plain on her face.

Sadie smiled at her new friend and shook her head. The last thing she wanted was for Jess to feel bad about the comment. She took Jess's hand from her shoulder and gave it a kind squeeze. "Apology accepted. You don't have to say another word. Honest."

As she held Jess's hand in hers, her heart beat faster in her chest. Sadie had the sense of becoming complete—as if she had found something that had been missing. She didn't want to let go and risk losing the feeling. She also didn't want to look like an idiot holding on to Jess's hand too long. She felt her cheeks flush hot again as she blinked to recover her senses and changed the subject. "So how about a beer? Then there's something I want to show you."

Jess gave a relieved smile and obliged, twisting the top off two bottles. "Something you want to show me? That sounds intriguing."

Sadie took one of the cold bottles and took a long drink, savoring the anticipation of her surprise for Jess. "Oh, it is," she teased as she linked her arm through Jess's and pulled her over to the machines she'd covered with a sheet earlier to extend the surprise. "Are you ready for this?"

"Am I ever." Jess played along. "I am *excited*, rock star."

"Close your eyes." Sadie squeezed her arm to encourage her.

"I'm not *that* excited."

"Come on." She squeezed again.

Jess rolled her eyes, but she followed instructions and let Sadie lead her across the floor into position.

"Okay, one…two…three…open!" Sadie yanked the sheet from the Ms. Pac-Man and Donkey Kong machines, but kept her eyes peeled on Jess's face for her reaction.

When Jess opened her eyes, she didn't disappoint. Both hands flew to her face to cover up her shock as her gaze ran over the pink and blue arcade game. "You have actual arcade video games in your house? That is awesome!"

"You can be Player One." Sadie started up the game as Jess set her bottle down and positioned herself in front of the joystick.

Sadie sipped her beer and watched as Jess expertly guided Ms. Pac-Man through the maze of dots, chomping away and avoiding the ghosts like a pro. It was nearly three full levels before Jess's luck ran out and Pinky finally cornered her, ending her turn.

"Player Two, you're up." Jess grinned as they switched places and Sadie grabbed hold of the controller. She took a long drink of beer making an approving grunt as Sadie maneuvered Ms. Pac-Man around the board escaping her pixilated foes. Jess cheered out loud when Sadie hit the points needed to earn an extra life. "Way to go! I had no idea you were such a top-notch gamer."

Sadie glanced over and caught the sparkle in Jess's eyes. Pride at the compliment mixed with contentedness that the two of them shared a love of retro gaming. "I don't know if I'd label myself a gamer. I'm only into these old-school, eighties arcade games like Pac-Man, Donkey Kong, Dig-Dug. My dad loved them when he was a kid. He's the one who got me into them. We used to come down here after dinner when I was in middle school and play until my mom would yell from the top of the steps that it was bedtime." She laughed, remembering how her dad would pretend to pout and beg. *Please one more game.*

"It's great that you two had that kind of relationship." Jess's eyes were kind as she laughed along with Sadie. "It's sweet that he shared things he enjoyed as a kid with you. That's a good dad right there."

Sadie nodded and continued to race Ms. Pac-Man around the board. "That he was. I miss him a lot." She blew out a breath to steady her emotions. She didn't need to get deep in her feelings about her dad in front of Jess. They were trying to have a game night, not a therapy session.

Luckily, Jess changed the subject, cheering on her game.

"You got the apple! Nice work."

"That will be the end of my fruit collecting. I can never get the melon without being eaten by a ghost." Her mouth formed a straight line as she shook her head. "I've given up on trying."

"You've given up?" Jess took a step closer. Sadie could smell her clean, soapy scent. "That doesn't sound like you. You're getting the melon tonight and I'm gonna help you."

Sadie laughed again. "You're going to help me? How are you going to do that?"

Jess set her beer bottle down and pressed against Sadie, wrapping her right arm around her, placing her hand over Sadie's on the joystick. "Like this. Is this okay?"

The heat from Jess's body sent a shiver up Sadie's spine. They hadn't been this close since that impulsive hug the night Jess gave her the Regina Phalange shirts. "It's totally fine."

"Good. Now, get ready. That melon is going to make an appearance soon."

Sadie did her best to keep her focus on the game, but her pulse was racing at the nearness of Jess behind her. Jess's breath was warm against her neck while she waited for the digital fruit to appear on the screen. Despite the sudden throbbing she felt between her legs, she kept her voice steady. "I'm ready for it."

"Here it comes. Follow my lead." Jess's hand guided Sadie's on the joystick, taking Ms. Pac-Man down the board to tuck into a neon corner of the maze. "Hold it here for a moment." Two beats passed. "Now go for it!"

Together the girls controlled Ms. Pac-Man, moving her quickly toward the melon, gobbling up dots as they went, until finally they reached their goal and got the fruit. An excited *whoop* escaped Sadie before she could help herself.

"I did it!" Sadie spun around to face Jess and put her arms in the air, triumphant. "I mean, we did it. Thank you."

Jess's hands slid to Sadie's waist sending another wave of excitement through her. "Now you know one of my best moves."

Even without the thick tone of Jess's voice, Sadie would have recognized the heavy-lidded lust in her eyes. "I'd like to know more of your moves." She licked her lips as her gaze slid to Jess's mouth. Her beautiful, plump lips were inviting as hell, and the small, barely visible freckle below the dimple in her cheek held incredible charm. Sadie suddenly had a strong urge to kiss her.

She leaned forward to make contact, but right before they connected a loud crash followed by her mother's yelp came from the floor above them.

"What was that?" Jess pulled back, her eyebrows raised in concern.

"Crap. I don't know." Sadie slid out of Jess's grasp and took off for the stairs. She called out as she went, "Mom, are you okay?"

When she arrived in the kitchen with Jess at her heels, she found her mother standing in the dimly lit room surrounded by pieces of a broken cookie jar on the floor along with the last of the chocolate chippers that had met an unfortunate fate.

"I was making tea and getting a cookie when the jar got away from me," her mother said with a frown as she gestured at the wreckage around them on the kitchen floor.

The girls sprang into action. Sadie hit the light switch and went for a broom while Jess collected the bigger pieces of jar and gingerly placed them in the trash can. The mess was cleaned up by the time the kettle whistled.

"Thanks girls." Sadie's mom switched off the burner to quiet the kettle. "Can I offer you some tea?"

"Thank you, Mrs. DuChamp, but I'm going to decline." Jess stuck her hands in her pockets and looked down at her feet. "I think I'm gonna call it a night."

"But we still have beers downstairs," Sadie protested. "We could play another game. I just learned how to get the melon."

Jess raised her eyes to meet Sadie's gaze. Although her expression was kind, it was clear she had made up her mind. "We'll do it again sometime."

Sadie walked her to the door and they said a quick goodbye before Jess slipped out into the dark summer night. She had hoped they would pick up where they left off downstairs and at least share a quick goodnight kiss, but that mood seemed to have shattered like the cookie jar that had interrupted them.

Had she imagined the sparks between them in the first place because she was caught up in the rush of excitement at beating another level of the game? Jess had definitely seemed as into the moment as she had been, and there was no mistaking the desire Sadie had witnessed in her eyes.

An exasperated sigh slipped from her as she leaned back against the foyer wall. Maybe it was for the best that Jess had gone home. Her mom had finally left her bedroom again and Sadie should be spending time with her, not chasing after the neighbor girl, no matter how much she longed to taste those beautiful lips.

But Jess had said they would do it another time. Sure, Jess meant they would get together for a beer, but maybe she meant they would have that kiss too. That same heat from earlier flashed in Sadie's core as she thought about Jess's hands on her waist and how close they had come to colliding in the most beautiful way.

Maybe next time.

# CHAPTER TEN

Sunshine streamed through the glass door in the kitchen late Saturday afternoon as Jess slid the big blade of the chef's knife through the block of cheddar over and over. It was going to be the perfect evening for an outdoor gathering. The knife she had hastily chosen from the wooden block on the countertop wasn't the proper one for the task, but it was getting the job done. The resulting pile of perfect cubes of cheese was a satisfying sight. She popped a piece into her mouth, telling herself it was in the name of quality control, before repeating the drill with a block of Muenster. Assembling the pasta salad was happy, mindless work which allowed her the opportunity to consider how she was going to handle the collision of worlds that was about to go down in her backyard at the party her mother was hosting for the neighborhood.

She had been doing what her mother had asked—being a friend to the girl down the street, whose summer was off to a rough start. That was really all she had been trying to do, but then the next thing she knew she was pressed against Sadie in her basement, the two of them working the joystick together. Then there was that almost kiss. Even thinking about it caused a shiver to slide down her spine. She tried to shake it off by focusing on her task—tossing the cheese into the big bowl of tri-colored pasta and setting to work chopping up a stick of pepperoni.

She and Sadie had made a good team as co-hostesses at the Queen of Hearts event the week before. They had worked well together, like she had reported to her mom when she got home that night. The next thing she knew, they were actually having fun, much more fun than Jess had ever had at one of those promotional events. Usually it was work but Sadie had made it pleasure. Jess had put through the rush order on those Regina Phalange shirts, called in a favor, and drove halfway across town to have them printed up as an attempt to make up for the crappy way she had acted that morning. Based on the way Sadie had looked at her that night when she saw the Ts—all sparkly-eyed and soft-smiled—it had been mission accomplished and well worth it. That look had set off fireworks in Jess's chest, and she wanted to earn that look again.

Therein lay her predicament: she was smitten, and she *couldn't* be smitten with this woman. She had to be friendly and courteous, and that was it. Their moms were friends and Sadie was practically a part-time employee of her mother's company. Plus, Jess still wasn't thrilled with Sadie starting this whole neighborhood mom rock band thing. *Nope.* There was a sensible voice in the corner of her mind reminding her that "just friends" was all it could be between them. That was why she had hightailed it out of the DuChamps' house that night they had hung out instead of staying for tea. She couldn't be smitten with Sadie, and she sure couldn't be kissing her in the basement.

Jess tossed the pepperoni along with some chopped-up veggies into the salad and tossed it in the dressing. She hadn't seen or heard from Sadie since she had left her house the night of their shared Ms. Pac-Man game, and now she was about to spend another whole evening with her. She swallowed hard against the flipping sensation in her stomach. She could handle this. She could be just friends with her. She didn't need to think about how it would feel to kiss Sadie's pretty neck or how sexy her toned legs had looked in that short tight skirt the night of the Queen of Hearts event.

"Hey, honey. That's looking good." Her mom was practically skipping through the kitchen as she plucked a bright red cherry tomato from the pasta salad and bit into it. She was already dressed for the party in a colorful sarong. Jess suspected the lift in her step was due in part to the Regina Phalange performance that was planned for the party. If only she could feel as gleeful and carefree about it as her mom did. Her constant social media monitoring had her on edge. "You know, it's not too late to reconsider this rock band thing for tonight. We've got a deejay. There's no need to put yourself out there like this."

"Jess." Her mother's voice was thick with warning. "We're not having this discussion again tonight. The show must go on. We've worked too hard to turn back now."

"Okay, okay." Jess surrendered as she yanked the bowl out of her mother's reach and covered it with cling wrap to get it safely into the fridge. It had been worth a try. "All ready to be the *hostess with the mostest?*"

"Yes, and I hope you're going to get in the spirit and put on something festive."

Jess set the tub of hardboiled eggs onto the counter and looked down at her outfit. Her mom had a point. A black tank top and cargo shorts didn't totally scream tropical theme, but she *had* added one detail to get in the mood. She fingered her necklace as she spoke. "I've got the puka shells on."

"I guess that's *something.*" Her mom sighed and planted a kiss on her cheek before pulling a deviled egg plate out of an overhead cabinet. "You know, the caterers are bringing plenty of food. You don't have to do any of this."

"I don't *have* to, but I want to. I think it adds a personal touch." That and prepping food for the party gave her something else to do besides worry about her mom participating in the whole rock 'n' roll fantasy. Damn it, who the hell did Sadie think she was, coming back to Tucker Pointe and planting that zany idea in the heads of the neighborhood ladies? These women were middle-aged moms, not rock stars. It was bad enough that her mom insisted on throwing a party for the whole neighborhood every year. She didn't need to get up and sing, making a scene in front of everybody. She needed to lay low and carry on as they always had. That modus operandi had worked for years, and there was no reason to stop. Her mom didn't need to take any chance that someone might notice her and connect her with—

"Hey ladies!" Shanna opened the glass door that led to the deck and let herself in. "Guess who's back and better than ever?"

Jess had worked with Shanna three times since the Friday before, so she had already witnessed her miraculous recovery from the stomach ailment that had plagued her. It didn't seem to faze her mom, and it didn't surprise Jess either. If there was one thing you could count on with Shanna, it was drama.

"Look at you." Her mom pulled Shanna into the kitchen and spun her around to check her out from all angles. "Now *this* is a festive outfit."

Shanna had dressed the theme to the max—grass skirt on her curvy hips, stacks of colorful plastic leis adorned her long, elegant neck, even a damn coconut bra on her…coconuts. Her long, amber brown hair had a fake hibiscus flower tucked amid the curls. The getup was completely over the top and did exactly what Jess suspected Shanna wanted it to do—get her right back into Marley Moran's good graces.

"I love a good theme, Marley. What can I say?" Shanna shrugged and shook her hips making the knee-length grass skirt *swish, swish, swish* around her legs.

Jess turned her attention back to her deviled eggs, carefully slicing each one in half and depositing the yolks in a bowl for further treatment. Her mom was too quick to trust people. Jess couldn't believe her mom wasn't going to at least comment on Shanna's sudden recovery. Sure, Shanna had worked for Queen of Hearts vodka for almost four years—since the summer after Jess's sophomore year of college—but that shouldn't excuse her from being called out when she pulled crap like faking an illness when she was most likely hungover. Her mom would never let it slide if Jess had pulled something like that.

As if she could sense Jess's jealous thoughts and wanted to soothe her—or possibly rub it in—Shanna squashed up against Jess and peered over her shoulder. "You cook?"

Jess clamped her mouth shut to keep an unfiltered response from escaping while she took a deep calming breath through her nose. Her mom wouldn't be thrilled if she couldn't keep a civil tongue while speaking to a member of the Queen of Hearts family. But did Shanna really have to make it seem like she could barely toss a salad together or prepare a simple appetizer? "Oh yeah, I'm not just a dumb jock."

"Huh. I was gonna go with more than just a pretty face." Shanna shrugged and gave her a wink. "But whatever floats your boat, Jess."

Jess bit back any further comment. She had learned over the years of working with Shanna that if you didn't ignore her more obnoxious moments, they would only escalate. Once the party was in full swing, Shanna would find someone else to get a rise out of. *Or…*

Shanna could be the key to Jess surviving the Sadie situation at the party. If Jess stuck by Shanna's side for the evening, she wouldn't be subjected to the eruption of butterflies in her belly anytime she was too close to Sadie—because she wouldn't get close enough to Sadie to let that happen. Instead, she would let Shanna's obnoxiousness run interference for her. It was a solid defense and the perfect way to maintain her "just friends" status with Sadie.

As Sadie approached the Moran house with her mom, both of them sporting their Regina Phalange shirts, her head was buzzing with excitement. She was looking forward to the party and seeing Jess again, but she was really pumped for the performance. It had been too long since she had played in front of a crowd. The anticipation had her amped up and she shook her shoulders in time with her footsteps to release a little excess energy. It was going to be a good night. She glanced over at her mom. "You ready for this?"

"Ready to play the guitar in front of people or ready to face a large social gathering for the first time in several months?" Her mother laughed nervously and grabbed Sadie's hand. "Truthfully? I don't know if I'm ready for either. But I'm glad I have you with me while I do it."

Sadie gave her a squeeze. "I'll be right by your side the whole time. Whatever you need."

The Morans' backyard was decorated in a luau theme—tiki torches surrounded the pool, fake palm trees had been brought in and dotted the landscape, and strings of lights adorned the rails of the deck. It was festive, and enchanting, and...romantic. The back of Sadie's neck tingled with anticipation as she surveyed her surroundings, hoping to catch a glimpse of Jess, but the blonde was nowhere to be found. At the far end of the yard a dance floor had been laid out as well as a small stage with the band equipment already in place, although a deejay was entertaining until it was time for Regina Phalange to make their debut. A crowd of jovial neighbors dressed in their tropical best was already getting the party started.

"This looks amazing!" Sadie leaned toward her mom so she could be heard above all the goings-on.

"Yes," she agreed. "Marley certainly knows how to throw a fabulous party."

Sadie couldn't argue with that, especially as Marley herself made her way through the partiers to meet them. Like so many of the partygoers, she was dressed to fit the theme—floral print sarong wrapped around her slim body, bright yellow hibiscus in her long, blond hair, a lei made of fresh flowers around her neck. She greeted them both with a hug and a kiss on the cheek.

"Who's ready to party?" she beamed. "We'll go on around nine thirty, so in the meantime, help yourself to food and hit the bar. Enjoy yourselves. Kristen and Sophie are at a table over there under a palm tree, so check in with them too. I think they're a little nervous about the whole Regina Phalange performance thing."

"They're not alone," Sadie's mom replied with a shaky laugh.

"Oh, come on." Sadie took her mom's hand with a reassuring squeeze. "We're going to be great. We are so ready for this." At least she was, and she couldn't do it without the rest of them. If she had to buoy the mood for the whole group, so be it.

"You better take that pep talk to palm tree number two over there. Light a little fire under the rest of Regina Phalange." Marley winked at her. "I'm with you, Sadie. I'm ready to go. I love a good chance to perform."

Sadie considered that as they strolled across the lawn. Marley was a great singer, and definitely got into her performance even when rehearsing. But Sadie couldn't help wonder where her love of it came from. Maybe she had been a singer in her past life when she was younger and before she had Jess? Sadie only knew of her life as their neighbor. Surely people changed and evolved as the years went by.

Kristen waved them over to the table. "Hey, girls." She was dressed in white capris and her Regina Phalange T-shirt with a multicolored lei around her neck, but Sophie—ever the sophisticate—was wearing a long, blue wraparound skirt and a white tank top with sparkly gems accenting the neckline.

Sadie sat down in one of the wooden folding chairs and plucked a grape off the plate in the middle of the table. Sophie started to tell a story about her kids and Sadie half listened while scanning the crowd of mingling neighbors in the yard. It wasn't until her gaze landed on Jess that she realized she had been searching her out again.

Jess was talking to an older guy whose belly was straining the obnoxious, Hawaiian print shirt he was wearing. Sadie didn't recognize him as a neighbor and assumed he worked for Marley. Jess didn't spot her right away, and Sadie took that chance to look her over. Her tight-fitted black tank made her skin look especially tanned, or maybe it was the tiki torch lighting that did the trick. She wasn't dressed for the theme of the party except for a puka shell necklace and flip-flops. Sadie couldn't be sure if that was intentional or not. When their eyes finally met, Sadie pointed at her Regina Phalange shirt and gave an exaggerated wink. A smile flickered across Jess's face, but she quickly broke the connection of their gaze and continued her conversation with big belly guy. A weird disappointment tugged at Sadie's heart. She didn't know what she had expected. She had thought they had bonded at least as friends the night they hung out, but it seemed Jess's moody self was back. The whole situation was impossible to read and left Sadie frustrated.

"Well, kids are like that." Kristen laughed with the other women at the table, and even though Sadie had missed the whole point of the story, she chuckled along with them to make it seem she had been paying attention, instead of obsessing over Jess.

"I think I'm going to grab a drink." Sadie finally excused herself and strolled toward the bar across the yard. She kept an eye on Jess, who was still involved in her conversation. If Jess noticed and cared that Sadie was on the move, she gave no indication.

Sadie ordered a vodka and cranberry from the handsome, dark-haired bartender with a flashy, super white smile, and when she turned back around, Jess was nowhere to be seen. It was as if she had disappeared into thin air.

The evening passed while Sadie mingled with the other guests, enjoyed the delicious buffet, and even hit the dance floor a few times. But her mind was preoccupied with thoughts of the upcoming performance and Jess. She hadn't resurfaced all night since that original sighting. Sadie was back at the bamboo bar cooling down with a glass of ice water when a tall brunette with long hair in spiral curls wearing a grass skirt sidled up beside her.

"Hi." One side of the woman's mouth hitched up into a suggestive smirk as her gaze ran down Sadie's body. "I'm Shanna. Are you from the neighborhood?"

The infamous Shanna of Queen of Hearts employ. She appeared to have recovered from the ailment that had kept her from working the night Sadie had filled in for her. She also seemed to be making up for her past transgressions with an over-the-top party outfit complete with stacks of dollar store plastic leis and a generous dusting of body glitter. Sadie gave her coconut bra the side eye, afraid to look directly at it lest a boob pop out. "Yeah I live down the street. I'm Sadie. My mom and I are friends with Jess and Marley. You work with them, right?"

Shanna nodded as she sucked down her tequila shot and waved at the bartender for another. "That's right. Queen of Hearts vodka is where it's at."

"Do you know where Jess has been all night? I haven't even had a chance to say hello to her." Sadie played with her straw and swirled it around the glass making the lemon wedge bob and the ice cubes tinkle. She had been taking it slow with the alcohol, not wanting it to impair her ability to play.

Shanna appeared to have been going strong all night, and she tossed back the second shot of tequila before answering. "I was hanging out with her inside before I came out for another drink. I'm sure she's around somewhere." Her words slurred slightly and she reached a hand up to adjust her coconut bra strap. "She works really hard for Marley. Jess is kinda obsessed with the company's social media if you ask me. It's too much. That's why things didn't work out between us."

Sadie's ears perked up at that. "You dated Jess?"

"Yeah. Well, no." She chased her shot with a big slug of beer, then sloppily licked her lips. "I came on to her really hard one night last summer and it didn't take at all. Like, who is going to turn this down?" She gestured wildly at her toned, big-boobed body, and nearly lost her balance on the barstool. When she righted herself again, her eyes went wide with inspiration. "Maybe she's intimidated by other strong women."

Or maybe she wasn't interested in a sloppy drunk who was employed by her mother. Sadie sipped her glass of lemon water. She didn't have time to worry any further about Jess's whereabouts. It was past eight thirty and she needed to regroup with the rest of Regina Phalange, so she excused herself and went to get ready for the set. But she made a mental note to revisit this whole Shanna and Jess thing, because one thing was certain: Jess hadn't spent a single minute with her all night, but she'd apparently spent plenty of time with Shanna.

Marley sauntered up to the microphone stand and cupped her hands around it before speaking. "Thank you all for coming. I hope everyone is having a good time tonight!" Her words were met with applause and hoots from the crowd, many of whom had gathered on the dance floor below. "And now one more treat for you—we are Regina Phalange!" She pulled the mic from the stand holding it up in the air and facing Sadie at her drum set.

At Marley's nod, Sadie clicked her sticks together and counted them in. "Two, three four!"

The band picked up the beat, filling in the sound, and Marley launched into the lyrics in her sultry voice. "I know you want a piece of this. But my heart you'll never get...."

Sadie pounded away at the drums, feeling herself let go and get lost in the music. She let the performance take over her body and mind and eased into her zen. Her worries about where Jess had been all night and the stress of how her mom was coping with things faded into the soft background of her consciousness. The beat she was banging out, the reassuring rhythmic strumming of the guitar, and the hyper trill of the keyboard became her entire world.

Marley held the attention of the audience, some of whom were dancing, as she strutted around the stage like a pro, singing their song. The band only had the one Regina Phalange original, and they would round out their set with covers of tunes the crowd would know to keep them hooked and pumped.

Sadie nodded to the beat and glanced around at the band. They seemed to be getting into the performance too. Even Sophie had changed into her matching Regina Phalange T-shirt and was bopping along to the bass line she was playing.

They were rocking it.

Adrenaline was running full force through her veins, and her heart pounded in her ears almost as loud as the rhythm Sadie was keeping on the drums as they segued into the next song on the playlist. It was a balmy evening and sweat rose on Sadie's hairline. She would be soaked by the time the set was complete. The thrill of the intensity drove her harder, wanting the partygoers to get the same kind of high. That was what it was all about for her.

The crowd was a sea of faces as Sadie looked it over, but there were a couple she managed to pick out. One was Shanna, although it wasn't her face Sadie noticed so much as her body slumped over the bar. She would be feeling that in the morning. The other face that stood out was Jess's. She had reappeared among the partiers, although she stood off to the side of the dance floor. Her long, lean body rested against a tree with her tan arms crossed in front of her. Her posture was guarded, but she was smiling. And looking right at Sadie.

She grinned back at Jess, too caught up in the music to control herself and play it cool. It was weird that Jess hadn't been around for a good part of the night, but she had come back to support Regina Phalange, and Sadie appreciated that. She didn't need to get tripped up by what was or wasn't going on between the two of them, or by whatever the deal was with Jess and Shanna. It didn't matter. Between her mom's situation and still being sworn off relationships after the crap with Corey, Sadie didn't need the additional drama in her life. All she needed was an occasional fix of rock 'n' roll and everything would be fine.

As she shifted her rhythm to match the beat of the last song, Sadie broke eye contact with Jess and focused on the music. She was drenched in sweat and loving the energy feedback from the crowd. A ton of people were filming them with their phones, a good sign the band was well received. Marley owned the performance and Sadie knew the whole experiment had been a success. A glance across the stage confirmed that even her mom was enjoying herself, grinning from ear to ear as she strummed her guitar. That glow Sadie had witnessed on her face after work the other day was back. The music was working its magic.

Regina Phalange struck their last notes and before the sound faded, the audience exploded with cheers and more applause. Marley motioned for the rest of the band to join her at the front of the stage, and as Sadie took her bow, she peeked over at the tree where she had seen Jess watching earlier. She was gone. Again.

"Thank you! Enjoy the rest of the night!" Marley's voice carried as the crowd dispersed. She pulled the band in for a group hug, all of the women beaming with the rush of performing. "That was awesome!"

"Yeah, Regina Phalange!" Sadie cheered and the other ladies laughed.

"It was a lot of fun," her mom agreed and kissed her cheek. "We should do it again sometime."

After the other ladies had packed up their instruments and gone off for refreshments, Sadie leaned against the bamboo bar and mopped the sweat off her face with a cocktail napkin. She motioned to the bartender to bring her a much-deserved beer. She wasn't ready to jump right back into the party after the performance, and she definitely wasn't ready to deal with drunk Shanna who was still propped up at the other end of the bar, so she took her drink and headed for some solace in the front yard. A little time to come down from the high would do her good, and since the crowd was all in the back of the house, the front yard was deserted. She sat down on the stone bench under the big dogwood tree and took a hearty swallow of beer before pressing the cold bottle to her forehead. The condensation mingled with sweat, and a cold drop slid down her face. She probably looked a wreck, but it felt damn good.

When Sadie first came back to Tucker Pointe and Kellie's posts with her new band back in New York started popping up on Facebook, she thought she might have to unfollow her lest she explode with jealousy. In the past couple of weeks she had forced it out of her mind—the way it felt to perform in front of people. The adrenaline rush that came from giving your all while a crowd looked on. The sweet balance of moving people with music while feeding off the energy in their response to it. The cheers, dancing, singing along—it all pushed her harder. She hadn't even fully realized what she had been missing until she felt it again. Maybe Regina Phalange would save her right along with her mom.

"You okay up here, rock star?" Jess's voice came from the darkness behind her, and even though it was soft and gentle as if in an effort not to startle her, Sadie still jumped.

She quickly lowered the bottle from her head, then swiped at the dampness still on her brow with her free hand, her heartbeat recovering from Jess's sudden appearance. "Yeah. I needed a minute to come down and cool off."

Jess nodded stiffly as she reached up and grabbed a thick tree branch above her head, not quite hanging from it, but leaning her weight against it. Her long, lean frame was illuminated by the house lights behind her. "You ladies were a big hit back there. It seemed like a lot of people were taking video on their phones. So that's...great." She smiled, but it didn't reach her eyes the way it normally did. Still, even with it at half wattage, her teeth looked especially white like an inner light was shining out of her.

Sadie's stomach did a little flip at the way that black tank top clung to Jess's form when she stretched. She had considered the people filming them a sign of success, but it seemed Jess didn't share her enthusiasm. "Thanks. It was a lot of fun."

They were silent while a car rolled by on the street. Voices and music from the backyard bounced off the houses, a whole different world compared to the peace surrounding them.

"You know, I think that was the first time I ever really saw you do that." Jess's brow dipped low and her mouth puckered as if she was really thinking about it.

"You've heard Regina Phalange playing in your basement." Sadie shifted in her seat, running her fingertips over the beveled edge of the bench. "So that's a big ol' lie."

Jess let out a low breathy laugh. "That's not the same thing. This was the real deal. Your total A-game."

Sadie liked that she had made Jess laugh. She wanted to do it again, but a strange shyness came over her. She dropped her gaze to her shoelaces and stuck with the truth. "No. Total A-game is when I'm up on stage pounding out song after song in front of a noisy crowd dancing and jumping around on the floor, moving almost en masse. And I'm dripping sweat and my hair is whipping around my face—even sticking to it—but I want to keep going for *one more* song because I know in that moment I am literally moving people. They are all following my beat."

When Jess didn't respond right away Sadie summoned the courage to look up again. She was staring at her like she was studying her. No longer smiling, Jess's face went blank. Sadie couldn't read her at all, so she rushed to fill the silence. "I'm sorry. I get a little passionate about it." Her lips involuntarily curved upward into a grin made by nerves. She took a swig of beer to rein it in. She kicked her flip-flops off and pulled her knees up to hug them to her chest, safe and cozy. The quiet moment stretched while distant party sounds from the backyard danced in the air around them. "That performance tonight felt good. It felt—I don't know—freeing."

Jess's brows knit together as if she was really considering Sadie's words and puzzling them out. "Freeing? Isn't that normally how playing feels?"

Sadie shook her head and chewed on the inside of her cheek. The adrenaline rush from performing had lowered her inhibitions, causing her to say more on the subject than she normally would. "It used to. I used to feel like this all the time when I performed. Before the obliteration of Sugar Stix. And before all the shit that happened with my ex, Corey."

"Two rough breakups." Jess nodded sympathetically. "I get that."

"They were rough," Sadie agreed. "I guess I didn't realize until tonight how much that stuff had been weighing me down all that time. You get used to carrying the weight of the world, you know? There was so long with Corey that—" Was she really going to admit this to Jess Moran? They had barely reconnected and here Sadie was laying her past on the ugliness table.

Jess seemed to sense her reluctance to continue. She ran a gentle hand down Sadie's arm. "I'm sorry. I didn't mean to bring up bad memories."

Sadie swallowed hard. She'd come this far, so she might as well keep going. Plus, there was something about Jess— something in her soft, comforting touch—that made Sadie feel like she could trust her. "No, it's fine. Corey was an addict. He hid it well for a long time. But his secrets destroyed him, and ultimately us. His behavior became…unbearable. He wasn't himself anymore. He became violent."

"He hit you?" Shock registered on Jess's face—her eyebrows raised, jaw dropped—and Sadie had to look away.

She tipped her face down, resting her forehead on her knees, too ashamed to answer the question.

"Sadie?" Jess tried again, but Sadie had said all she was going to say on the subject. The past was in the past.

Sadie squeezed her eyes shut to reset her thoughts and an embarrassed laugh bubbled out. "I'm sorry, that was a bit of an overshare. Music does that to me. I pull a lot of emotions out of it. Makes sense since I pour so much of myself into it." Heat rose in her cheeks against the cool evening air. "I'm all over the place right now. I must sound like a total freak."

Crickets chirped playfully in the darkness, and for a moment, the women stared at each other, comfortable in the quiet moment.

"Beautiful." Jess finally spoke and that word slipping through her lips made Sadie's heart skip a beat. "Your passion, I mean. It's a beautiful thing. I can see it in your eyes when you talk about making music. You're lucky, not everyone has that kind of thing in their life."

Sadie's pulse pumped even harder as she realized Jess wasn't describing her looks, but her drive. She ran a hand through her hair, forgetting about the flower she had tucked behind her ear earlier until she knocked it out of position.

As it dropped to the ground, Jess reacted, kneeling down in the grass to retrieve it from under the bench where it landed. The muscles in her back flexed under her tank top as she grabbed for it and Sadie's whole body flushed warm as she enjoyed the view.

"Here you go." Jess remained down on the ground and offered the bloom to her.

As Sadie took it, their hands brushed against one another and she lifted her gaze to see if Jess had noticed, but she was studying Sadie's face again. Their eyes locked and Sadie swallowed hard. Her brain reeled, searching for something to say to bring them back to normal—that place where they were laughing and joking around. And where she wasn't thinking about how it would feel to kiss Jess's big, sexy mouth.

It was Marley's voice calling out across the yard that finally broke the spell. "Jess? Are you up here? I need your help bringing out more food."

"Be right there." Jess slowly got to her feet, eyes still focused on Sadie. "Duty calls."

Sadie tucked the flower back behind her ear and rose from the bench to stand as well. "Yeah, you better get going."

"Right." Jess stared into her eyes a beat longer. Sadie sucked her bottom lip between her teeth to keep her mouth from doing something it might regret. Jess reached out and slid her fingertips down the length of the tattoo on Sadie's shoulder. "Catch you later, rock star."

Jess dragged her flip-flops and bit her bottom lip as she ambled across the yard to the house. She shoved her hands into her pockets, hunched up her shoulders, and willed herself not to look back at Sadie. She needed to decompress from the way her body heated up after spending time in Sadie's orbit. If she looked back she would never recover in time to appear normal in her mother's kitchen.

Missed opportunity—that's what it was. They had been so close. So close to finally taking the plunge and pressing their lips together. Closing her eyes, she recalled the scent of Sadie's honey mint lip gloss. She had been so close to tasting it. God, how she had wanted to taste it.

It was like they had been under that tree together forever. Sadie's eyes were the color of sunlight filtering through the overhead trees, and when Jess had looked into them, she became lost and mushy. It was like she was racing through a tunnel with the rest of the world blurred into oblivion. Nothing else mattered but the two of them. Being with Sadie left her dizzy and giddy and disoriented with the rush of the experience. Her fingertips had been drawn to that tattoo on Sadie's shoulder like some kind of magnetic pull, and damn if she didn't sense a jolt of electricity searing through her at the contact. It was like nothing she had ever felt before. It was some sort of weird sex magic. Maybe Sadie had put her under a spell.

Jess shook her head at the ridiculousness of the thought as she closed the front door behind her and blinked against the bright lighting of the foyer. It was a stark contrast from the dusky summer night. She had to push those sappy thoughts about Sadie out of her head. They were friends. And possibly part-time coworkers. But really, that was it. It was a good thing her mother had summoned her when she did. She had spared Jess from doing something foolish. *Get it together, Moran.*

Her mother was buzzing around the kitchen refilling trays with cheese and crackers, pita chips and dips, and other supplies to keep the party going even though it was almost eleven o'clock and the crowd was starting to thin out. "So, what did you think of the set?"

Jess chewed the inside of her cheek. The practical, social media expert side of her had a lot to say about it, but she knew that wasn't what her mother wanted to hear. "The band was great and everybody loved you. In fact, they loved you so much they took videos. I mean, there were a lot of cameras in that crowd."

"Oh, Jess, people were just having fun."

"Mom, you have no idea how fast social media can work. Things go viral faster than you would believe."

"Honey, no one cares about a bunch of middle-aged women singing in their backyard. I promise you're worrying about nothing. Now, help me out and throw some mint in that pitcher and muddle it for another batch of Vodka Mojitos. Simple syrup and lime are in the fridge." She pulled a bottle of soda water from the pantry and set it on the counter before scooting to an overhead cabinet for more cocktail napkins.

"Is the lime vodka on the cart?" Jess asked, but her mom's answer floated right by her as the scent of the fresh mint grabbed her focus. She closed her eyes and breathed it in. Immediately she was pulled back to that time spent with Sadie in the front yard. The delicious honey mint of Sadie's lips and how fucking close she came to kissing them.

"Jess! Muddle, not destroy." Her mom's stern voice snapped her back to reality.

She eased up on the mint and went to the fridge for the other ingredients. The cold air could help her chill out from the memory of Sadie.

And as far as the "just friends" thing went—Jess was going to have to try a lot harder.

# CHAPTER ELEVEN

Sunday evening Sadie hummed along to the jukebox and leaned against the bar and waited for her last table to leave. In order to take Saturday off to attend Marley's party, she had agreed to work both lunch and dinner service at her job at Lenny's. It had made for a long day of serving pizza and pitchers of beer, and she was ready for her shift to be done.

She stared blankly out the big storefront window of the restaurant and replayed the Regina Phalange performance. It had felt damn good to play in front of people again, even if it had only been a neighborhood party in the Morans' backyard. She was also pleased that her plan to boost her mom's spirits had worked. She and the other ladies had been all smiles for the remainder of the night at Marley's. Not that Sadie had stuck around for much longer after she and Jess had their quiet moment out front. She had left the party on a good note before things between her and Jess could come crashing down like they always seemed to.

It was too bad that night was probably going to be it for Regina Phalange. It had been one thing when they had the goal of a performance at the party as a reason to get together and play, but with that behind them, the neighborhood ladies would probably go back to coffee dates and coupon swaps whenever they got together. All it had taken was those few songs in front of people for Sadie to get the itch to perform again. If that was how she felt after less than a month in town, it was going to be a damn long year in Tucker Pointe.

She sighed and glanced over at her one remaining table in the otherwise empty restaurant. The couple seated there appeared to be on a date in the early stages of the relationship. There was a lot of smiling between them and some nervous napkin tearing going on under one side of the table. Dessert dishes had been cleared; drinks were still half full. Determining that she could be hanging out for a while, Sadie hitched her butt up onto one of the stools and took a load off.

"Damn it." Michael, manager on duty and grandson of the original owner of Lenny's Pizza, dropped his phone down on the bar behind her and put his hands behind his head, elbows in the air, as if he was surrendering. "What is it with people not being able to keep commitments? Is it *that hard* to do what you say you're going to do?"

"Woman trouble?" She reached over the bar, grabbed a maraschino cherry from the garnish tray, and sucked it off the stem.

"Worse. The band I had booked for Thursday night canceled. They said there was a miscommunication and their manager double-booked them, or some bull crap like that. Now I have to find a decent replacement in four days. Fuck me."

Sadie's eyebrows rose, her jaw dropped, and her pulse kicked into overdrive. Michael was in need of a band, and she had an itch that playing in front of a crowd could scratch. Adrenaline released into her bloodstream thinking about mentioning Regina Phalange to him. What if he outright laughed at her? Michael did that sometimes. He was cocky, and since his grandfather owned the joint, he thought he was pretty big stuff. Plus, she couldn't really promise him anything until she talked to the other ladies. That would be the fair thing to do. But if she didn't say something, she could miss out on the opportunity altogether. In the end, the showman in her won out. "I might be able to help you with that."

"What?" Michael spun to face her, hands still laced at the back of his head as he squinted his eyes suspiciously. "You gonna fly your old band out here to play Thursday night?"

Sadie bit back a laugh at how ridiculous the thought of that was. She had only received a couple of texts from Kellie since moving home, and she hadn't heard from the guys at all. A Sugar Stix reunion tour was not likely to occur any time in the near future. "Actually, I have a new band I've been playing with." He didn't look completely convinced. "It's all chicks."

His face brightened at that. "An all chicks band, huh?"

"Yep." She nodded enthusiastically, then felt a little guilty about not giving full disclosure. "I mean, they're all in their late thirties or forties. They're…my mom's friends."

Michael had released his grip on his head and was now stroking the stubble on his chin. "Cougars, huh? That's hot."

She bit the inside of her cheek and nodded, not trusting herself to respond without her repulsion at his reaction slipping out. The man was her boss after all, and she wanted the gig.

He squinted at her again. "You think you can fill the Thursday night slot?"

"I'll check with them tomorrow morning and have an answer for you by noon."

"No later. My balls are to the wall here." Michael frowned and scratched at his ear.

"Lovely expression, Michael. Noon it is."

"Neighbor girl, huh?" Cassie's voice slid up an octave as it came through Jess's phone. She was clearly delighted at the revelation. "That sounds like a pretty sweet setup for the summer. And I saw the backyard concert on YouTube. Five thousand hits is damn impressive. Your mom looks incredible, by the way."

Jess was beginning to regret calling her best friend to see how things were going back in Cincinnati. It was Sunday night, and although they had exchanged text messages, she hadn't actually talked to Cassie since leaving the apartment. Jess had seen the high number of hits that YouTube post had received over the weekend, and the last time she checked, it was still on the rise. Then there was her new friend Sadie. Of course Cassie would assume she was on the prowl for a summer fling. "It's not like that. She's been helping out my mom so we worked together. It's not like *a thing*."

"The more you say it's not *a thing*, the more it actually sounds like it's *a thing*." The shoulder shrug came through in Cassie's tone. "So, you like her. That's great."

"No, it's not great," she argued. "I mean, I don't like her."

"You just went on for fifteen minutes straight about how hot she looked the other night playing the drums. You *totally* like her."

"God, Cass, I think you've been reading too many of those romance novels while you're waiting for your mold spores to multiply. Sadie and I are just…."

The sound of her mom talking to someone downstairs caught her attention and derailed her train of thought. That *someone* sounded a hell of a lot like Sadie. Jess poked her head out of her bedroom door to get a better listen. Snippets of conversation floated up to her.

"…sorry, but I had to come tell you right away…too excited…think the rest of Regina Phalange will do it?"

Were they seriously making future plans for Regina Phalange?

"You have *got* to be kidding me," Jess growled.

"Hello? Jess?" Cassie's voice came through the phone. "Are you still there?"

There was no time to explain to Cassie. She had to get downstairs and put a stop to whatever zany scheme Sadie was trying to talk her mom into this time. "Sadie's here, Cass. I'm gonna have to call you back."

"You like her!" Cassie's taunt came through the line before Jess could click off the call.

Jess shoved her phone into her pocket and hopped down the stairs to get to the kitchen where her mom and Sadie were working themselves up into a full whirlwind of rock 'n' roll fantasy excitement.

"A real gig? Like at a bar?" Her mom was gushing like a teenager. One of her hands was on Sadie's shoulder, and the other was covering her mouth as if she'd had the surprise of her life.

"Absolutely not." Jess stomped her running shoes against the tile floor. Suddenly the room felt like it was spinning. "You cannot do that."

"Jessica Rose." Her mother spun to face her. "Are we really back to this again?"

"Mom, playing for the neighbors in the backyard was one thing, but at a bar? No way. You cannot do that." She shook her head vehemently. She was not giving in this time. "This is exactly what I was afraid of when you guys started this whole band nonsense."

Sadie flinched at the word *nonsense* and her excited expression dropped. Her gaze met Jess's, but her eyes were full of hurt. "Why would you want to take something that makes us happy away from us? Why would you want to steal our joy? Does it make you feel good to do that?"

The accusation stung and Jess's stomach lurched in shame as she realized how she sounded. Sadie didn't understand. She couldn't. "I don't. I mean, that's not what I'm trying to do." She chewed on a cuticle. She wasn't trying to insult Sadie or Regina Phalange or anybody. "I'm sorry. I shouldn't have said that. The band sounded awesome when you played at the party. It's just that my mom shouldn't—"

"Your mom is a grown woman who can decide for herself what she should or should not do."

Her mom stepped between them and gave Jess a meaningful look. "Can I speak to you in the other room for just a moment?" She didn't wait for an answer before grabbing Jess by the arm and dragging her out of the kitchen. "Sadie's right. I can decide for myself, thank you."

"Mom, someone posted the backyard concert on YouTube and it got over five thousand hits. Do you get what that means?"

Jess rubbed her temples. How could she make her mom understand? "That's a lot of eyes on you. And Queen of Hearts was tagged, so it's not that big a jump to assume someone will make the connection if they recognize you as…" Her gaze flicked toward the kitchen where Sadie was still waiting, not that far from earshot. She sighed and lowered her voice. "You know how trolls on social media can be. We've dealt with them enough."

"I'm not making this decision lightly. It's a risk I'll take. Regina Phalange has been good for Jennifer, and we're all having a good time together. We're rallying for a friend."

Their gazes locked, each silently daring the other to back off. Jess wasn't ready to give in, but her mom's hands-on-hips stance made it clear she wasn't backing down either. Her mother was a real force when she wanted to be. The sound of Sadie clearing her throat in the kitchen was an awkward reminder that an answer needed to be made one way or another. Jess closed her eyes and shook her head. The fact was they were a team, but her mom was the team captain. She had the final say. If she was going to insist on living on the edge, it was Jess's job to keep her from completely tumbling over, despite her ill feelings about it. What other choice did she have? "Okay. I guess you should give Sadie your answer."

"Playing at Lenny's sounds like fun, and if the rest of the ladies in Regina Phalange want to do it, I'm in," her mom announced as they reentered the kitchen.

"Great." A fraction of the original smile returned to Sadie's face, although she seemed to be avoiding eye contact with Jess. In fact, she was ignoring her altogether and getting right back to business where the conversation left off. "We'll need to plan some practices."

"I'll talk to the other ladies first thing in the morning so you can give an official answer to Michael," her mom said evenly, but excitement still plainly showed on her face. "I'll leave persuading your mother up to you." She gave Sadie's shoulder a sweet squeeze as she walked by, but all Jess got was a warning look clearly meant to convey she had some apologizing to do.

With only Sadie left in the kitchen, an awkward silence settled over the room. Jess knew she had hurt Sadie, but she honestly hadn't meant to. She was so accustomed to looking after her mom that she wasn't used to factoring in the feelings of anyone else. That had obviously been a mistake.

Jess was familiar with Lenny's Pizza. The place had been a staple in Tucker Pointe as long as she'd lived there. It really was more of a family restaurant than a bar, and she'd eaten there dozens of times with her mom. Would it really make that big of a difference if her mom got up and sang a few songs? It was a neighborhood joint, not some big nightlife hot spot. Most of the people there would probably be people from their party the weekend before anyway. Plus, if Regina Phalange played another gig, it would give Jess another chance to see Sadie rocking out on drums. There was something almost magical about the way Sadie lit up when she was pounding away in front of a crowd. Thinking about it caused a stir of heat in Jess's chest that slowly creeped up her neck. Sadie was always beautiful, but when she was in her element like that in front of an audience, she absolutely glowed. It was like Sadie had said when Jess barged into the kitchen—it was her joy. Witnessing that again was surely worth the tiniest bit of risk that came with Regina Phalange playing one gig at Lenny's Pizza. But still...those YouTube hits. *Ugh*.

"Well, I guess I'll get going. It's been a long night." Sadie finally broke the silence and sighed as she turned to leave.

Jess snapped out of her reverie and quickly followed her to the front door. "Wait. Don't go. I want to..." What did she want? To hang out with Sadie? Touch her? *Kiss* her? "...apologize."

"You already did." Sadie shrugged, but paused in the doorway.

"I know, but I want you to know it was sincere. I know it probably seems weird that I'm so protective of my mom, but she...." She couldn't explain her reasons to Sadie or anyone else even if she wanted to, so there was no point of going down that road. She slid into her usual excuse. "It's always been the two of us and I guess we've formed some habits over the years. But seriously, playing with Regina Phalange has made my mom happy—all of the women seem happier to be honest. You have a real gift."

Sadie's shoulders relaxed and the full smile returned to her face. "Thank you. That's sweet. But these women are doing something they enjoy. It's not anything I did."

"It is," Jess insisted with a firm nod. She stepped closer to Sadie who was now leaning back against the doorjamb. You're the one who introduced them to the joy. You totally did this."

A laugh like a hiccup burst out of Sadie. "You know, the last time you said those words, it was more like you were blaming me. Which is it? What are you trying to say, Jess?"

She placed her palm on the wall behind Sadie and leaned in as close as she dared. She searched Sadie's face for a sign that she should back off, but she came up empty. If she was going to make a move, this was as good a time as any—before she made another stupid comment and accidently insulted Sadie again. Their bodies were a mere fraction of an inch away from pressing together and heat zapped between them. Her voice was low as she finally replied. "I'm saying that I can see things from a different perspective now. And I really like what I see." Her gaze was trained on Sadie's lips as they parted, but whether it was to speak or an invitation to kiss her Jess would never know because Sadie's phone beeped in her hand causing them both to jump and breaking the spell that had fallen over them.

"It's my mom." Sadie stared at the screen and tapped out a reply. "I didn't tell her I was stopping here on my way home and my shift was done an hour ago. She's wondering what the hell happened to me. See?" She looked up to grin at Jess. "I understand how mothers and daughters worry about each other."

Jess took a step back to put some space between them. Her brain recognized the moment had passed, but her body was still buzzing from the close encounter. A little distance couldn't hurt. "So, I guess you should go." *Please don't go.*

"I should." Sadie looked down at her tennis shoes before meeting Jess's gaze again. "I'll call you tomorrow, though. Maybe we can hang out."

It would have to do. Jess waved before watching Sadie disappear into the shadows between their houses on the street, but she was already looking forward to that call.

# CHAPTER TWELVE

On Tuesday morning Jess popped a coffee pod into the machine and leaned back against the kitchen counter while she waited for her drink to brew. She was going to need a hearty mug of caffeine to fuel the morning ahead.

She hadn't expected the call from Sadie on Monday evening to be a request for her to babysit, but that was what she got. Kristen had agreed to rehearse with the other women of Regina Phalange, but she had to bring her kids with her. That meant someone had to keep an eye on them. Jess didn't really think that babysitting was an activity roadies did regularly, but Sadie smartly insisted that for Regina Phalange roadies it was.

Stirring a spoonful of creamer into her mug, she laughed remembering how excited she had been when she saw Sadie's number pop up on the phone. Then there was the very persuasive tone of voice Sadie had used while assigning her duties for the Regina Phalange practice. Jess had fallen for it hook, line, and sinker.

No matter. If keeping an eye on Topher and Mia for a bit while the band rehearsed was what it took for Jess to show Sadie she could be supportive of Regina Phalange, then babysitting was what she would do. They were cute kids, and it was the least she could do after the way she had upset Sadie the other night. Still it was for a good reason…

She held the hot mug in her hands and blew across the surface before sucking in a sip, enjoying the peace of the morning while she could.

It didn't last long.

Her mom rushed into the kitchen, fastening a chunky silver chain bracelet around her wrist. "Can you pop one of those in for me, hon?" She nodded in the direction of the coffeemaker. "I can't be late for this. Sadie needs me."

Jess rolled her eyes at her mother's dramatics, but did as told and started her mug of coffee. "Sadie needs you?"

"I may have spoken too soon when I said everyone would be on board with this gig at Lenny's. Sadie said Jennifer was up for it, but Kristen and Sophie require a little more convincing." She paused to blow out a breath as if trying to keep herself calm. "They agreed to come today, but I'd be lying if I didn't say they were more than a little reluctant. I never should have promised Sadie without checking with them first."

"You were trying to be supportive of Sadie. And Jennifer. It's only this one gig at Lenny's. They'll get through it and Regina Phalange can hang up their guitars for good." She tried to focus her attention on the positives of the situation and not her concern about her mother fronting a band. She might have agreed to bite her tongue regarding her feelings about the upcoming gig, but that didn't mean she would stop worrying. She'd been all over the Internet monitoring for any signs that the backyard concert video was getting the wrong kind of attention. "You know, I keep an eye on other social media, not just Queen of Hearts, and the rumors of …*your friend* still being alive and well are buzzing again."

Her mom nodded as she took her mug from the machine and added a scoop of sugar and a splash of cream. "I know you're worried, Jess. But those rumors are cyclical. They pop up every couple years and then they die down again. This isn't any different than the last time they surfaced."

Jess bit back her response about the difference being they had the Queen of Hearts twentieth anniversary gala to plan and she already had enough on her plate without wrangling Internet trolls too. At least she was getting to spend more time with Sadie. "I guess."

Her mom put a hand on Jess's shoulder and gave it a squeeze, breezing right over Jess's worry. "Like you said, this gig is a one-time thing. Kristen and Sophie will be fine. By the way, it was nice of you to agree to look after Topher and Mia."

Jess grinned. If her mother only knew how she'd been roped into it. "I don't mind at all. I'm happy to help out with whatever Regina Phalange needs. In fact, did you hear Sadie officially made me a roadie?"

"A roadie, huh?" Her mom smiled that *I think I know too much* smile. "You and Sadie certainly seem to be getting on okay."

"Yeah, we're…" Jess racked her brains for the appropriate word that could possibly define their relationship, but in the end she dumbly repeated her mom's words. "We're getting on. Don't worry, Mom, I'm being a friend to the girl down the street like you asked me to." That was the truth, or at least the easy part of it.

Yet, with every passing day, Jess was finding herself more and more attracted to Sadie. There was no reason to get into all of that with her mother, though. She wasn't ready to discuss her feelings with anyone else. She was still trying to figure it out for herself. Two days ago Jess was adamantly against Regina Phalange playing at Lenny's. Now she was an actual part of the operation and the thought of Kristen and Sophie bailing on Sadie at this point was practically unthinkable.

She shook her head and downed the last of her coffee. "If you're so worried about being late, we better get going."

Her mom made an agreeable noise and drained her mug. "Do you have what you need for the kids?"

Jess nodded. "I already made a couple of runs over to the DuChamps' this morning with supplies, as well as band equipment for Regina Phalange. I'm going to grab a couple things on our way out."

The two of them headed out through the garage where Jess snagged a soccer ball and orange practice cones. Obstacle courses had always gone over well with Topher and Mia when she sat for them in summers past. She would pull out every trick in the book to keep the kids occupied if it helped make the Regina Phalange rehearsal go smoothly for Sadie.

"Please help yourselves to the fruit and bagels. The coffee will be ready in a minute."

The way her mom buzzed around the living room made Sadie's heart happy. Her mom had set out a decent breakfast spread for the ladies of Regina Phalange—behavior that was much more like her old self—another sign that the band was good for her mom.

As Sadie poured Topher and Mia cups of orange juice, she stole another glance at the door. The sooner Jess got there, the sooner they could get this rehearsal started. Once they were actually playing music, she would relax. Kristen and Sophie had agreed to come over and play, but she had a nagging feeling they weren't completely convinced Regina Phalange was ready for the great wide world of Lenny's.

Before she could stress too much over it, Marley came in through the front door followed by Jess, who looked like she was starting a new career as a phys. ed. teacher, right down to the whistle she wore on a lanyard around her neck.

"Who wants to play with water balloons?" Jess called out as she marched through the living room. The kids followed her like the Pied Piper and she winked at Sadie as she passed her on the way out to the backyard.

Sadie couldn't help but smile back at the impromptu parade. She didn't know what had sparked Jess's new attitude about Regina Phalange, but she was grateful for the change of heart. If Jess could keep the kiddos busy long enough for the ladies to get through their song set, it would help the cause. She certainly looked like a woman up to the task.

It was a relief when the band finally took up their instruments and started practicing the set. They played through the first two covers without incident, but when it came to the Regina Phalange original, "No More," they barely made it through the first verse before they were knocked off beat and the song fell apart.

Sadie smacked her sticks against the tom-toms stalling out with the rest of them. "Whoa, what happened there?" She tried to keep her voice light. Regina Phalange was made up of neighborhood moms, not rock 'n' roll professionals.

"Should we take it from the top maybe?" Marley turned to face the drum set and address Sadie.

Sophie glanced across the group at Kristen who cleared her throat and played with a dial on her keyboard.

"What's happening?" Sadie asked again. "Is something wrong?"

Sophie set her bass down with a sigh and picked up her mug of coffee. Everyone stayed silent and all eyes remained on her until she set her mug back down. "Maybe we are in over our heads," she finally said with a shrug.

"Over our heads?" Sadie dropped her arms to her sides. A sharp pain took root in between her shoulder blades. She had believed Marley's reassurances that all the ladies would be on board, despite the nagging sense in the back of her mind that they might not all be as enthusiastic as she was about the Thursday night gig. But there it was, the seed of doubt taking root and blossoming at an alarming rate.

"You know," Kristen chimed in, "this gig at Lenny's is the real deal. We're just some suburbanite moms from the cul-de-sac. Sophie's right. We might be in over our heads with this."

"Lenny's isn't a big deal," Marley protested. "I think it's going to be a lot of fun. Plus, they're paying us fifty bucks each to show up and play, and that's a LOT of clipped coupons!"

Michael had been agreeable to giving them what he would have normally paid the regular band, which made the thought of backing out of the gig even more gut twisting to Sadie. She would never live it down at work.

"Playing covers in your backyard is one thing, but playing in front of a bar full of strangers…" Sophie shook her head. "I don't know if we can do it."

Sadie's heart sunk. Regina Phalange was an all-or-nothing proposition as far as the members went. There was no band without Sophie and Kristen. And if there was no band, Sadie would have to come up with a whole new way to pull her mom out of her funk, not to mention she would have to break the news to Michael that he had an empty stage for Thursday night again.

To her surprise, it was her mom who spoke up. "We can definitely do this." Her voice was as firm as the nod of her head when she said it. "I know we can do it because we already did. This is the same music, the same instruments, the same Regina Phalange that performed in Marley's backyard. It doesn't matter if we're playing in front of five people or five hundred. Sophie, remember how you sent that group text after Marley's party about it being the best time you've had in ages? Let's grab a little more of that joy. Our ability is solid. We can do this."

"She's right." Marley picked up the rally cry. "We all deserve that kind of joy in our lives. Let's get back to practicing and show them how it's done."

Sadie looked from one woman to the next. She didn't want to steamroll anyone into doing something they weren't up for, even if she felt desperate to have Regina Phalange perform again. "Sophie and Kristen, are you okay with this?"

The two exchanged a look and to Sadie's relief, an understanding seemed to pass between them.

"Sadie, if you think we can do it, I'm in," Sophie confirmed.

"Me too," Kristen seconded it.

"Then let's get back to it." Without further discussion, Sadie raised her sticks above her head. She gave the women a moment to pick up their instruments before counting them in. "One, two, three, four!"

The second time through "No More" went much smoother and the band moved on to the next song in the set. By the time they got to "Bad Reputation," Jess and the kids had come back inside and were jumping around, dancing to the music.

Sadie looked around the room as she pounded out the beat and beamed with satisfaction. Everyone was smiling and having a good time. Her chest filled with pride and she felt the stress from earlier drain from her shoulders. The plan was back on track. Regina Phalange was back in business.

# CHAPTER THIRTEEN

From the moment Sadie clicked her sticks in the air to count them in Thursday night at Lenny's Pizza, the crowd was rocking with Regina Phalange. The band covered songs that fit their brand—"I Hate Myself For Loving You," "Love Bites," "Gives You Hell"—Marley's voice putting her polish on them. The customers at the bar ate it up, singing along, and some even got up to dance on the tiny dance floor in front of the stage.

It was Sadie's total A-game, like she had explained to Jess that night in front of the Morans' house. Her gaze searched the room seeking out Jess as she pounded through the chorus of "Thnks Fr Th Mmrs" until she finally spotted her leaning against the far wall across the bar, nodding in time to the music. She flashed a smile as Jess gave her the double thumbs-up before she became consumed by the performance again.

As the band transitioned into their last song—an amped up version of "You're So Vain," Sadie noticed a tall, dark-haired guy at the front of the crowd, staring at her with a flirty grin on his face. She bit her bottom lip and smiled back, relishing the moment of showmanship. He kept his gaze locked on her as they drove through the verses of the song. Sadie twirled her sticks in the air before hitting the last cymbal crashes of the piece, and seeing she still held his attention, gave him a wink before rising and taking a bow with the other ladies.

As the cheers died down and Michael took the mike to thank the crowd again, the band gave one last wave to the audience and set to work putting away their instruments. Sadie pulled her sweat-soaked T-shirt over her head as she broke down the drum set and packed it up. Working in her sports bra would be a lot cooler. Before she even got the cases open she heard someone calling out to her from the edge of the stage. "Hey, drummer girl."

She turned and saw the guy from the last song waving at her. Still high on the performance, she continued to play the part of rock star and sauntered over, tucking her T-shirt into the back pocket of her cutoff jeans. "What's up? Did you enjoy the show?"

"Very much. You girls rock." He stuck his hand out. "I'm Dan."

"Sadie." She shook it. The word 'girls' used to describe a band made up of the neighborhood moms made her smile. She would have to remember to pass that one on to the other ladies. "Thanks, Dan. Thanks for coming out tonight."

The way he continued to beam at her fueled her performance buzz. It was like for one moment she was famous, which was ridiculous. Playing at the pizza joint where she worked part-time was hardly a prime gig. More like a one-off. On the other hand, a fan was a fan, and she would enjoy it while it lasted.

"Your lead singer was awesome. I swear I know her from somewhere." He scratched at the stubble on his chin. "Is she… nah. Forget it."

"Is she what?" Was he trying to ask if Marley was single? Jess would probably go nuts.

"Nah. I'm just imagining it." He shrugged and waved a hand like he was dismissing the thought. "Are you going to play here again?"

"I don't know. Maybe. So keep your eyes open for us." Sadie placed a hand on his shoulder and gave him one last bright smile before ending the interaction and turning her attention back to dismantling her drums, kneeling down on the stage beside them to get to work.

"What the hell was that?"

Clearly Sadie was not going to be allowed to handle the task in peace. Jess's neon pink running shoes at her side was the first thing Sadie saw, and she swallowed hard as she dragged her gaze up her jeans and plaid collared shirt to her face, not looking forward to what was coming next. Jess's stance was rigid with her arms crossed. Her expression was plainly stern—eyebrows pinched together, mouth in a tight line. She was pissed off.

"What the hell was what?" Sadie stood up so she was at full height too. If Jess was about to bitch her out for something there was no way she was going to take it while kneeling in front of her.

"That thing with that guy back there. Do you even know him? And you're walking around in your…" She had uncrossed her arms to wave her hands in front of her, gesturing at Sadie's body. "Bra."

Sadie whipped the sweaty T-shirt out from her back pocket and tossed it at Jess who refused to react. It hit her squarely in the chest and dropped to the floor. "My shirt was soaked and it was plastered to me. Would you prefer I walk around like a contestant in a wet T-shirt contest?"

"I'd prefer you walk around in *something*. And maybe not fawn all over random guys who hit on you. Sleazy and desperate is not the image Regina Phalange is going for."

"*Fawn all over?* I barely touched him. And what the fuck do you mean *desperate?* I was being polite," she hissed, fighting to keep the volume of her voice low. Who the hell did Jess think she was? The exchange had caught the attention of the other women packing up their instruments, and her mom's eyebrows rose in concern. Heat crept up Sadie's neck into her cheeks. "And sleazy, seriously? You're our roadie, not the morals police. You're not even a real roadie. God, I can't even." She shoved past Jess and strode out the side exit into the cool evening air. The post-performance buzz she had enjoyed earlier was shot to hell, leaving her feeling let down and grumpy. The last thing she wanted to hear in that moment was the slam of the door as Jess joined her outside.

"Sadie—"

"Leave me the fuck alone." She leaned her mostly bare back against the rough brick of the building's exterior and wrapped her arms around herself, shutting Jess out.

"I'm sorry." Jess wasn't that easily put off. She stood in front of her and scrubbed at her face with her hands. "Please let me explain."

"Explain what?" She spat the words out and refused to make eye contact. Her stomach roiled. She knew better than to let her guard down for someone, but she had done exactly that with Jess. "That you think you're in charge of me because we let you help out with Regina Phalange?"

"*Let me help out?*" Jess's voice turned as hard as Sadie's; all traces of apology were gone. "I make this little hobby of yours easier for all the other women you dragged into it."

*Little hobby.* The sour words echoed off the far corners of Sadie's brain. Sure, she enjoyed playing with Regina Phalange, but the whole reason she started the group was to help her mom, and everyone else had been on board. She had made certain of that. Jess had some fucking nerve suggesting that she was being self-serving with the band. "Right. You make things so much easier by hanging around with us and calling me sleazy. What the hell is wrong with you?"

Jess's hands balled into fists at her sides, and for a moment Sadie thought she was going to scream. Instead, she took a deep breath that sucked some of the bravado out of her posture and tucked her long hair behind her ears. "Nothing is wrong with me. I feel like it's my responsibility to protect you. Not only you. My mom is part of this group too."

"The group I started because I was looking out for *my* mother. Damn it. We can't keep having this same fight. We both want to take care of our moms. Got it." Sadie pinched the bridge of her nose, willing herself to calm down. Apparently both she and Jess had their mothers' best interests at heart. Although why Jess's mother, a grown woman, needed to be protected was beyond Sadie's realm of understanding. They were on the same team, and there was no need for a knock-down, drag-out screaming match about it in the back alley of her place of employment. "You have no right to freak out because I talked to someone. That's not you protecting me from anything. It's just you being a jerk."

Jess looked down at the ground and kicked at some loose cinders on the asphalt. "It wasn't the talking by itself." She frowned. "It was the winking, and mugging, and lip biting. You were *flirting* with him."

"It's part of the act, Jess. It doesn't mean anything. And, even if I was flirting with someone, what do you care?"

Her gaze snapped up to meet Sadie's again and she took a step closer. Sadie could feel the heat off Jess's body as much as she could see it blaze in her eyes. "Don't you get it? It absolutely kills me to watch you enjoy other people's attention, tease them, flirt with them, whatever. Because one of these days you're going to want to kiss one of them. And that will tear me apart." She was so close that her breath was on Sadie's lips, a mix of beer and mint gum. "Because that's all I've wanted since that first day I saw you swimming in the pool—to kiss you."

Sadie's heart pounded in her ears as Jess's words registered in her head. "You wanted to…."

"I expected to come home for a quiet summer helping my mom with her business, getting things lined up for my last semester at school, maybe working on my tan in my free time. Instead I find you—this gorgeous, bold, independent woman— swimming in my pool. And the next thing I know, you've shaken up my whole world. I'm letting my walls down, I'm a fake roadie for a rock band, and I can't get you off my fucking mind." If she had more to say, she didn't get the chance because Sadie pulled Jess to her and sealed their lips together, kissing her hard and urgently.

Jess's rigid posture relaxed into Sadie as she pushed her up against the wall. Her hands went to Sadie's waist, holding her as if to make it clear she had no intentions of being interrupted this time.

Sadie tangled her hands in Jess's hair as she parted her lips to allow Jess's tongue to slide against her own. A tingle slithered down Sadie's belly at the sensation, like something finally waking and coming to life inside of her. She grabbed on to Jess tighter, afraid that if she let go the moment would disappear the way the mist of a dream left in the morning.

She slipped one hand down Jess's neck to her strong shoulders, urging her on, wanting her hands all over her, but as Jess responded by sweeping her fingertips over Sadie's hips to her ass, the side door to the bar slammed again. Jess let out a low growl as she stepped back and their warm bodies broke apart. The cold air was a shock against Sadie's bare skin.

Marley walked out followed closely behind by that guy Dan who had questioned Sadie earlier.

"You just look really familiar," he was saying to her back. Marley was doing a damn good job of ignoring him. "Maybe you have a sister or something?"

"What the hell, dude? First you hit on my girl and now my mom?" Jess scowled. Dan held his hands up in surrender and backed down the alley away from the women. Clearly this was not his night for a love connection. "Yeah, show's over. Get outta here."

Marley exchanged a smug look with Jess. Her cheeks blushed as she stood with her hands on her hips and shook her head at the girls. "I guess you two worked it out, whatever that was in there. When you're ready, the rest of us are all packed up," she said simply before disappearing back into the bar.

The same mix of surprise and desire coursing through Sadie seemed to be reflected in Jess's face as they stared at each other. Her heart was still pounding, quite possibly audible in the sudden, still silence between them.

"That was, um…." Sadie stammered.

"Awesome?" Jess supplied, wrapping Sadie's hand in her own and rubbing a thumb across her fingers until Sadie grabbed onto her.

Sadie looked up with a bashful smile despite the fact that she had been ready to jump Jess's bones moments before. "Yeah. That."

Jess ducked her head and kissed Sadie once more, this time soft and sweet. "Come on, we better not keep our moms waiting. Musicians can be total divas."

She rolled her eyes and laughed at Jess's smartass expression as they headed back inside. The rest of Regina Phalange was going for coffee, but Sadie wanted more of Jess. They couldn't walk away after what had happened between them when they were outside, at least she couldn't anyway. She needed to know what this meant for them. She'd kissed Jess, and Jess had wanted to be kissed. After all the moods and the back and forth, Jess had been jealous when Sadie talked to some random guy. She had shut her feelings down so much that she had totally missed the signs and now she needed to know more. When Jess offered her a ride home, she gladly accepted.

There was an obvious shift in the mood as they loaded Sadie's drum cases into the back of Marley's SUV. The brief time with their mothers and the other women had shaken the vibe between them. Sadie's body was still humming from Jess's warm touch, and she ached to have it again. She glanced over as Jess lifted the last two pieces of the set and slid them into the back of the vehicle. Jess's slim body stretched and a hint of skin showed from under her plaid shirt as she reached up to close the tailgate. A stirring began in Sadie's core as she remembered Jess's fingertips sliding across her hips.

The slam of the trunk stopped her mind from wandering down the path of *if only*. The hot moment between them in the alley could have been nothing more than the culmination of emotions working themselves out. Maybe it hadn't been real at all. When their eyes met once more, everything clicked back into place and Sadie's insecurities fell away. She recognized the lust in Jess's heavy-lidded gaze. She sucked in her breath and waited for her to set the pace.

"I guess we should get going."

"Yeah."

Jess sucked her bottom lip between her teeth, and her eyes searched Sadie's face as if considering something. "Would you like to come back to my house? I mean, for a drink or whatever?"

*Yes! Yes! Yes!*

"Sure." She slid into the passenger side of the car and they were off.

By the time they reached the house they had fallen back into the easy banter they had known earlier. Before the fight. Before the kiss. Before Sadie was so damned confused about what was going on between them.

Jess parked in the driveway and led her to the gate at the side of the house. The pool was lit up and the water had a peaceful glimmer across the surface. Sadie focused her gaze on it, trying to quiet her racing mind. They walked toward the back of the house, but Jess stopped suddenly halfway to the sliding door and turned back to her.

"Sadie, what happened back at the bar, you know, between us?"

"The...kiss?" She fixed her gaze on Jess's mouth as she spoke the word and hoped she meant the kiss. The mere thought of the two of them tangled up in each other in the alley filled her with warmth.

Jess reached for her, running her fingertips along Sadie's jawline before they came to rest on her chin, tipping her head up and forcing their gazes to meet. Her expression was soft, the light behind her casting a halo effect around her beautiful face. Sadie held in her breath, willing Jess to kiss her again. "I want you to know I meant what I said. I've wanted to do that since the minute I laid eyes on you. Resisting has been making me crazy." Jess's posture shifted and she leaned in.

*Do it again. One more taste. Show me it's for real.* Sadie silently begged as she closed her eyes anticipating the sweet contact. But right as she felt her breath on her skin, she felt an uncomfortable fluttering at the back of her head that she suspected wasn't Jess playing with her hair. More like a...*bat!* Instinctively she slammed up against Jess for shelter from the creature, catching the other woman completely off guard and forcing her to step to the right to steady herself. Unfortunately, since they were standing right next to the pool, there was no solid ground for her foot to land on. Jess's eyes flew open in panic and she waved her arms in the air trying to regain her balance, but it was in vain.

As Jess pitched toward the water, Sadie grabbed her forearm, but she was too far gone and the effect of gravity was too strong to reel her back in. As Jess slipped from her grasp Sadie was pulled along by the momentum, and she splashed down into the pool beside her.

"Damn it, rock star."

Sadie came back up to the surface of the water to see Jess slicking her long, wet hair back out of her eyes. "Oh my god. I'm so sorry," she sputtered. "There was a bat!" A glance at the dark sky confirmed her concerns were not her imagination as the animal made another swoop over the pool. She grabbed on to Jess again, their wet bodies pushed together. Jess's hard nipples pressed against her, and a shiver slid through Sadie that had nothing to do with the cool night air.

Jess's arms wrapped around her, holding her close. Protecting her. "How does this keep happening to us?"

"I don't know, I—"

Before she could finish, Jess's mouth was on hers, kissing her with the hunger she had seen in her eyes earlier. Sadie cupped her cheek in her palm as Jess slid her tongue between her lips. They could only make out while treading water for so long, but Sadie never wanted the moment to end.

Jess squeezed her tighter in her arms before breaking off the kiss. "You're shivering. Let's get you into some dry clothes."

Sadie's focus went to the thin, soaked layer of fabric that separated their skin. She was still only wearing a sports bra, and their nearly bare breasts rubbed together. Heat creeped up in her cheeks, and she bit back a self-conscious giggle. "Okay."

Jess released her and they pulled themselves out of the pool onto dry land once again. She grabbed a couple towels from a plastic trunk at the edge of the patio, and while she rubbed at her hair with hers, Sadie wrapped herself in one like she was the filling in a cozy burrito.

She followed Jess through the house and up to her room where Jess went straight to the tall, cherry wood dresser and rifled through it for clothes for the both of them.

It was funny how similarly empty their "home" bedrooms were. A navy blue duffel bag sat in the far corner of the room. It looked as if Jess might be living out of it, much like the suitcase still on Sadie's floor at her house. And there was no extra clutter on the furniture either, like what collects when you spend a long stretch of time in one place. None of that, "I emptied my pockets right here and forgot about it" stuff like movie ticket stubs or packs of gum, or mementos from nights out. The bare minimum.

Sadie's hair was beginning to dry misshapenly, and as she stood in front of the mirror combing her fingers through it, trying to push it into its regular style, she eyed up the few things on the surface of the dresser. There was a mug with the Queen of Hearts logo on it full of coins, a half empty bottle of perfume, and an old photograph that had tattered edges and bent corners. She picked it up and flipped it over, but there was no date or indication of when or where it was taken.

She studied the picture and smiled at the chubby-faced little girl looking out of the shot. "Is this you? Did your mom have brown hair back then?" She squinted to reconcile past with present. "Marley went through a goth phase. Who knew?"

"What?" Jess looked up from the drawer she was digging around in. When she noticed Sadie was holding the photograph she strode across the room and peered over her shoulder. The sigh she expelled tickled Sadie's neck. She hesitated before commenting, "It's uh, it's an old picture."

"Clearly." Sadie handed her the photo, trading it for the shirt and boxer shorts Jess had pulled out of the dresser for her. "Look how cute baby Jess was." She wanted to make her laugh, but Jess kept her eyes trained on the picture and chewed on her bottom lip seemingly lost in thought.

After a beat, Jess finally spoke again. "It was a long time ago." She looked up, eyebrows pushed together as if considering something. "In fact, it would probably be best if you didn't mention anything about seeing this picture to my mom. She'd probably be embarrassed that I let anyone lay eyes on it."

"Really?" Something about Jess's mood shift seemed weird. It was just a photo, and Marley was such a cheerful person, Sadie couldn't imagine that she would embarrass that easily. Everyone looked weird in old pictures with dated fads. But she didn't recall seeing any other pictures from when Jess was a baby around the house, so maybe Marley really did want to leave her goth style buried in the past. "Okay, of course. I won't say anything. Promise." She leaned in and kissed Jess's cheek.

The smile returned to Jess's face and her eyes swept down Sadie's body as she pulled back. Sadie suddenly remembered the dry clothes she held in her hand but had yet to put on. "Hey, don't be getting any ideas. I have to go home. I need a good shower and some sleep."

"Too late." She shook her head. "I already have lots of ideas. More than one of them include a shower, but none of them involve sleeping."

Sadie giggled at Jess's lopsided grin and gave her a playful shove in the shoulder. It wasn't that she didn't have those same ideas taking root in her mind about the beautiful woman standing in front of her. Even though Jess's long hair hung wet around her face, and she had droplets of water dotting her lashes and cheeks, her eyes shone a bright sapphire blue and her lips were plump with a juicy sheen—tempting and completely kissable. But she and Jess had gone from rocky friendship to fighting to…well that, all within a span of eight hours. Suddenly her head was spinning with emotions, and even though her body was still buzzing from kissing Jess, she needed time alone to process everything before rushing into anything more. She twisted her features into a serious expression and fixed Jess with a hard warning stare.

In response, Jess shrugged with a playful, "Can't blame a girl for trying" grin and left the room to give her privacy. Sadie quickly changed clothes before joining her in the hall, still stunned yet pleased by the turn the night had taken. She was really starting to like Jess, but she wasn't ready to let things go off the rails. She'd been a fool in this department before. In spite of the way the blood pumped through her veins, causing a mighty strong pulse in certain parts of her body, she had to slow things down for the night. They had the whole summer to see where things went next—no need to rush it. "Walk me home?"

"Absolutely."

# CHAPTER FOURTEEN

When Jess had texted her Friday night mid-shift at Lenny's and asked her out on a real date for Saturday, Sadie had been quick to say yes. She couldn't wait to spend a whole day together not working, not doing Regina Phalange stuff, just hanging out together and getting to know one another better.

But Saturday morning as the metal guard arm slammed shut across their seat on the carnival ride known as The Orbiter, and Sadie tightened the feeble canvas strap that served as a seat belt across their laps, she wondered if she should have been a little less enthusiastic about agreeing to this outing. She placed her hands on the thick metal bar in front of her. "Are you sure this thing is safe?"

"Sure it is." Jess laughed and put her hand on top of Sadie's. "You can relax your death grip. I'm not going to let anything happen to you. I thought you said you'd been to a carnival before."

Sadie kept her eyes locked on the teenager running the ride as he fastened a chain to block off his control booth. "I have. My dad used to bring me almost every summer when I was a kid. I guess I was a lot more fearless back then."

Jess dragged her fingertips across Sadie's knuckles as the ride started up. "You got this. Hang on. Here we go!"

The car moved forward on its circular path before spinning on its axis causing the girls' hips to bump against each other as they slid across the seat. Sadie's heart was in her throat and she curled her fingers around Jess's, holding on for dear life.

Jess let out a whoop and gave her a reassuring squeeze. Her long blond hair whipped around her face as the car spun again and she sputtered against a strand of it that stuck to her. Despite that, the look in her eyes was pure joy.

As the car completed its first loop and the girls' hips bumped again along with the motion of the ride, Sadie couldn't help but giggle.

"I heard that. You're having fun, right?" Jess called over the whirl of the machine. "Come on, let it out."

"Let what out?"

"One of these." Jess threw her head back and let out a long, loud howl.

Sadie laughed in earnest and a tickle of excitement worked its way up her spine. As they spun again she joined Jess with a howl of her own.

"That's the way. This time with hands up." Jess raised their intertwined hands in the air and their joyful voices rose in unison before they both dissolved into giggles.

As the ride finally slowed to a stop, tears of laughter were leaking from Sadie's eyes. She clambered out of the car and discovered her legs had turned to jelly. She grabbed onto Jess's arm for support which caused a whole new wave of laughter to overtake them.

"I need to find my sea legs." Sadie gulped air, recovering from the giggles.

Jess patted her hand and pulled her away from the ride. "You realize we're on dry land, right?" She teased with a grin. "Don't worry, I've got you."

Sadie's head was still spinning as Jess led her to the midway where barkers called out from games of chance. She was relieved to have a moment to recover. "You want to try your luck with one of these?"

"You pick." Jess squinted as she surveyed the row of booths. "Anything but the guess your weight one. That's a little too much information for a first date."

"Please." Sadie gave her a wry look before running an appreciative gaze over the length of Jess's body. "Whatever you say. How about the ring toss?"

"Perfect."

The girls approached the booth and Jess paid for a bucket of little plastic rings to throw at the grid of glass soda bottles lined up on the ground below them. The girls took turns tossing rings and cheering each other on. After many unsuccessful throws, Jess finally managed to ring a bottle.

The barker hit a button under the edge of the booth and an alarm sounded. "We have a winner! Pick a prize."

Jess rubbed her chin as she eyed the prizes hanging at the back of the game. "I think you should pick." She turned to Sadie. "I'm guessing you're going to go for that blow-up guitar, rock star."

"Well, you're wrong. I'll take the stuffed bunny." She thanked the attendant as he handed over the two-foot-tall hot pink rabbit. She hugged her prize and raised an eyebrow at Jess. "It's so cute and fluffy. I couldn't resist. Plus, there's more to me than just rock 'n' roll."

"I'm starting to pick up on that." Jess linked their arms as they left the games behind them. "What's next? How about the Ferris wheel?"

Sadie shielded her eyes from the sun with her free hand and looked up at the tippy-top of the big wheel. Her stomach did a flip, but she swallowed hard and gave Jess a nod. "Let's do it."

With her big bunny on one side of her and Jess on the other, Sadie leaned back against the vinyl seat of the car of the wheel, closed her eyes, and drew a long breath in through her nose. It had been a long time since she had ridden amusement park rides. As much as it reminded her of happy times being a kid, she couldn't help but recall shocking stories she had seen on social media over the years about people dying on these rides.

As the wheel began to move to allow the next party to load, Jess slid an arm around Sadie's shoulders. "Are you afraid of heights?"

Sadie shook her head. "Afraid? No. Not unless I get too inside my head about it."

While the other cars were loaded up, Sadie gazed at the park below her. Everywhere she looked there were people walking hand in hand, excited kids being chased by parents from attraction to attraction, revelers enjoying the sunshine, and the thrill of a day at the carnival. She turned her smile to Jess, who was grinning back at her. Their gazes locked and Sadie felt a jolt of electricity tear through her, setting off a flutter of butterflies in her belly. She glanced at Jess's lips and leaned closer longing for the additional thrill of a kiss from the beautiful girl beside her, but she paused short as a grinding noise came from the Ferris wheel and it made a sudden, jerky stop. She sat back up in her seat as the blood rushed out of her head. "What the hell was that?"

"I'm sure it's only a hitch in the ride and we'll be moving again in a minute." Jess's voice was calm as she rubbed Sadie's shoulder, but her eyes darted to the ground below, betraying her true level of concern.

"Oh god, we should have never got on this deathtrap." Panic rose in Sadie's chest as she sucked in breath after breath.

"Babe, it's going to be okay. You've got me and Big Bunny here with you, and this is a momentary pause in the action," Jess cooed. "Didn't you say you used to come to the carnival when you were a kid? Did you ever ride the Ferris wheel back then?"

Sadie nodded and swallowed, her throat suddenly dry. "I did. Me and Dad would ride everything. Mom wasn't so great with anything that spun around. When we would ride the Ferris wheel, she would watch and wave from the safety of the ground below." She peered cautiously over the edge of their car, but quickly snapped back to an upright position in her seat. "My mother is a very wise woman."

"We're fine. This is nothing more than a slight glitch." Jess shook her head before changing the subject. "So your mom is doing okay? I know she'd been keeping to herself more than usual since your dad…"

"It's okay." Sadie gave a half smile. "You're right, my mom had cut herself off from everyone. That's part of why I thought Regina Phalange would be good for her—get her involved in something again, you know?"

"It seems like she enjoys playing with the band."

"I think she really does." Sadie could feel the adrenaline from fear pushing her into overshare mode again, but she kept talking anyway. "When I came home from New York and realized the state of things for my mom…I felt really guilty. After my dad died I needed my music to help me through the grieving process. I itched so bad to get back to my band and play. I…think I left my mom alone too soon. I should have stayed with her." Tears stung at her eyes as she uttered the confession. "Sorry, I don't think I've said that out loud before."

Jess put her hand on Sadie's thigh and gave it a gentle rub. "You don't have to apologize for talking about how you feel. I'm glad you want to tell me about it."

The car shook again and Sadie gave a start, her heart jumping in her chest. "Is this thing ever going to move again? We've been up here for like an hour!"

"It's been maybe five minutes," Jess reassured her. "Let's talk about something else. Ask me anything and I'll answer."

Sadie bit her lip and considered Jess's offer. There was one burning question that had been plaguing her since the neighborhood party. "Is it true that you and Shanna used to date?"

Jess jerked back, eyeing Sadie as if she had grown a third tit. "Me and Shanna? Hell no."

"Ever hook up with her?"

"Double hell no." Jess laughed. "Truthfully? I've never had a real relationship before this."

Sadie's brain floundered for a response. It wasn't that Jess hadn't had a relationship before. It was the end of the sentence that had her speechless. *A relationship before this.* Meaning what they had was a—"You want a relationship with me?"

Jess's eyes went wide. "I thought that's what was happening here. I didn't mean to overstep, but that's what I'd like. I feel like it's the direction we're headed."

A chunk of stress melted from Sadie's shoulders as she stared into Jess's sapphire-blue eyes. "That's what I'd like too." She leaned in again, determined to seal their words with a kiss, but suddenly the big wheel jolted, then began its regular motion again jostling the girls in their seat. A cheer went up from the other passengers on board and both Sadie and Jess joined the celebration, leaving the kiss for later. Sadie's heart continued to beat in her throat until they exited the ride.

Once back on solid ground, Jess took Sadie's hand and led her through the park toward the exit. "I think we've had enough adventure for the day. What do you say we get something to eat?"

"We're not going to feast on corndogs and cotton candy?" Sadie teased.

"I thought for lunch we would class it up a bit."

Twenty minutes later, they were pulling into street parking down the block from Lenny's Pizza. Jess parked the Jeep then quickly scooted around the vehicle to open Sadie's door for her. "Don't worry, I'm not taking you to Lenny's." Jess offered her hand to help her down to the curb. "I thought we could eat at the Bloom Café."

Sadie continued to hold on to Jess's hand as they started down the sidewalk toward the cute little café with outdoor seating in the sunny garden adjacent to the building, but as they got closer to the restaurant it became apparent something was amiss. There was a crowd gathering out front and a firetruck on the far side of the café. The girls walked faster, curious to see what was going on.

"Look, there's Kristen." Sadie pointed to the edge of the group. "Maybe she knows what's happening."

Jess waved to Kristen as they approached. "Hey, looks like we missed something."

Kristen returned the wave and Topher, her four-year-old, ran toward them.

"Miss Jess!" He threw himself into Jess's arms as she scooped him up off the ground. "We saw a firetruck!"

"You did?" She carried him back over to his mother who had her daughter Mia, clinging to her leg.

"Oh yes," Kristen confirmed after greeting the girls. "We've witnessed a good deal of excitement here. Kitchen fire apparently."

"So much for our Bloom Café lunch plans." Jess shot Sadie an apologetic grimace before turning back to Kristen. "Did everyone get out okay?"

Kristen nodded. "They got everything under control pretty quickly. I don't think they'll be serving food for the next couple of days, but they'll recover."

"And I got ice cream!" Topher announced.

"I see that." Sadie laughed and rubbed the curly brown hair on the top of the kid's head. "I think you're wearing a good bit of it."

Kristen pulled an apologetic face. "Ugh. Sorry about that, Jess."

"Don't worry about me." Jess rubbed at a smudge of chocolate on her neck as she lowered Topher back down on his feet. "A little ice cream never hurt anybody. But we do need to get something to eat. I promised Sadie lunch and we've had a long morning."

They said their goodbyes and the girls headed back to Lenny's. As they entered the pizza parlor, Jess rubbed her hands together and made a face.

"I think I better take a minute and wash up before we order." She frowned. "I'll be right back."

As Jess headed past the row of diehard day drinkers at the bar on her way to the ladies' room, Sadie wandered over to the ancient upright piano against the far wall of the dining room. She sat on the bench, stretched her back long and straight, and flexed her fingers above the ivory keys, shaking away the nerves about playing piano in front of people. It wasn't her strongest instrument, but she knew enough to pick out a tune. When she wrote songs she mostly used a guitar to sketch out the music because that was what she normally had on hand.

She wiggled her fingers before curling them over the keys as she had been instructed in the lessons she had taken as a child and plunked out a few experimental notes. A quick glance over her shoulder confirmed not a single day drinker at the bar gave a damn about what she was doing. She pressed down again, this time with more confidence, fully forming the chords to the intro of the new song she had been working on since the day she popped out of the pool and spotted Jess Moran standing there.

She closed her eyes and thought about the lyrics. A picture formed in her mind of Jess holding her hand on the Ferris wheel and comforting her. Taking care of her. It had been a long time since someone had done that for her, and it felt damn good. The seed of love for Jess had planted itself in Sadie's heart, and with every passing day, it bloomed a little more. That was what had inspired the song she was playing. By the time she reached the chorus, she was caught up in the music and relaxed enough to sing along out loud.

With you, I'm bigger, bolder, better, your love is like a sweater
Worn in warming me to the core
With you, awaken all my senses, your love it leaves me breathless
Thick and thirsty begging for more
With you, I'll take the chance
With you, my life's a dance
Without you I don't know what I'd do
I'm much more me when I'm with you

Jess swore she heard music, and as she exited the bathroom, she realized it was her date sitting at the piano singing slow and sweet about love. It was a side of Sadie's music she hadn't heard before, and Sadie's tender words warmed her heart. Every day she learned something new about her, and every day she found herself hungry to learn more. Sadie had rock 'n' rolled her way into Jess's life, and she was one hundred percent hooked. It was clear from the way her instinct to protect Sadie had kicked in at the carnival earlier. Then the whole relationship thing—the word had slipped out before she could stop it. But for the first time in her life, she felt like that was the right word for what was happening. Something had shifted between the two of them over the past week, and suddenly she couldn't imagine her life without Sadie.

She didn't dare speak until the last chord faded. "I thought you only wrote rollicking rock songs and angsty anthems."

Sadie startled and jumped in her seat. "They're my go-to, but sometimes other feelings manage to slip out."

"That song though…that was beautiful."

Sadie spun around on the swivel stool to face her. "Not as beautiful as the girl I wrote it about." A blush spread across her cheeks as she stood and took Jess's face in her hands. "I meant what I sang. I'm much more me when I'm with you."

The song was about her. Sadie wrote the song for her. Impulsively, Jess grabbed her by the hips and pulled them together. Her heart pounded so hard in her chest, Sadie had to have felt the beat against her own. She sucked in her breath, closed her eyes and met Sadie with a kiss that was hard and greedy and full of the fire in her heart.

This was what she had been missing—not the kissing, she'd had plenty of that—but the connection she shared with Sadie. A buzz ripped through Jess at her touch. It energized her with a spark that sizzled right down her spine. She suspected the connection wasn't based on attraction or how dreamy the kissing was alone. It was what you got when you found the person you could open up to and truly be yourself. And it was something Jess never wanted to lose.

They broke off the kiss when the regulars at the bar hooted at them. Heat rushed to Jess's cheeks and she let out a giggle as they pulled apart, embarrassed that the tender moment had been witnessed by a pack of strangers.

"Oh sure." Sadie shook her head. "*That* they notice."

"What?" The kiss must have caused that old sex magic to fog Jess's brain because Sadie's words weren't making a damn bit of sense to her.

"Never mind." Sadie grabbed her hand. "Come on, let's get out of here."

"But I owe you lunch."

"Screw lunch."

They stepped back out into the afternoon sun and Jess walked Sadie to the passenger side of the car, but instead of opening the door, she pulled Sadie into her arms again. "Now, where did we leave off in there?"

"Mmmm." Sadie peppered her neck with delicate kisses as she spoke. "Somewhere right...about...here."

As their lips finally met, Jess backed her up against the Jeep. Their bodies joined together as she slid her tongue into Sadie's mouth. Her nipples went hard under her thin tank top and she let out a moan. "You have no idea how badly I want to throw you in the back of this car and fuck you."

Sadie worked her hands under Jess's tank and her fingertips found her breasts. "Believe me," she growled. "I do."

Jess nibbled along Sadie's jawline. "Get in." She bit out. "In the back."

Sadie fumbled with the door handle, but managed to yank it open. Jess pushed her down against the leather bench seat. Sadie grabbed a fistful of Jess's top and pulled her down on top of her.

"God, you're so sexy." Jess ran her tongue along Sadie's bottom lip and kissed her again. She slid her hand up her thigh, under her dress, boldly pushing on the lace of her thong.

Another moan escaped Sadie, a hot hiss against Jess's cheek, but then her eyelids fluttered open as if good sense was battling back in her brain. "Fuck. Jess, wait."

"Which is it?" Jess paused her hand from its ascent to Sadie's pussy. "Should I fuck or wait?"

Beneath her, Sadie let out a throaty laugh before kissing Jess firmly but quickly on the mouth. "We can't do this here. Damn it. I want you, but we can't do it here."

Jess blew out a long breath as she shifted and propped herself on her elbow to take some of the weight off Sadie. "Okay, I know, I'm sorry. You're a classy girl who deserves much better than a quick finger bang in the back of a car in a public parking lot."

Sadie's throaty laugh sent another burst of butterflies through Jess's core. "That's not exactly what I meant. It's just that we're outside my place of employment, getting it on in broad daylight."

"Fair point."

"But there's still something I need, and I think you know exactly what it is." Sadie's voice dropped to a sexy register and she rested her palm on Jess's cheek. "How about we take this back to my place?"

I think that's an excellent idea." Jess wasted no time waiting for further instruction. She planted a quick kiss on Sadie's lips, climbed out of the car, and rushed around to the driver's side.

Sadie did her one better and scrambled straight from the backseat over the center console to the front. As Jess started the car, Sadie slapped her hand on her thigh, digging her fingertips into the flesh there. "And Jess, drive fast."

Once inside her house Sadie locked the front door behind them, shutting them off from the rest of the world. They held hands and giggled, practically tripping over one another in their haste to get up the steps.

Jess paused at the top of the staircase. "Your mom's not home, right?"

"No. She went shopping with Sophie," Sadie said over her shoulder as she pushed through her bedroom door. Sophie had insisted on dragging Mom to the big mall. The drive there alone was thirty minutes. They would have the house to themselves for hours. She looked around for the lighter she had left on the bedside table the night before to light a couple of candles. Just because she was desperate to get naked with this incredible woman didn't mean all sense of romance and style should be tossed out the window.

"What are you doing? Get over here." Jess pulled her into a kiss, this one hard and urgent. She found the zipper on Sadie's dress and made quick work of pulling it down and slipping the garment off her shoulders.

At the same time Sadie got busy on the buttons on the front of Jess's shirt, her excitement growing with every pop. With the blinds drawn to keep the sunshine out, the flickering of the candlelight cast a surreal glow on the couple as they kissed and touched and teased. They stripped until Sadie was left in her thong and Jess in her bra and boxer briefs.

Sadie dragged a slow finger down Jess's front, over the curve of her breast, along her breastbone, across her tight abs, before finally coming to rest on her hip bone. She sucked in air as she reacted to Jess's creamy, soft skin under her touch. A shiver slithered down her spine and her pussy clenched with want. She tangled her hands in Jess's blond hair and stepped her backward to the bed. "You're so damn beautiful." She moaned against her between kisses as they tumbled onto the mattress.

"And you are sexy as fuck," Jess growled and straddled Sadie, effectively pinning her legs to the bed.

Another burst of excitement let loose in Sadie's core like butterflies on steroids. She sat up, quickly releasing the clasp of her bra with one strum of her finger. Jess's nipples beaded as the air hit them and Sadie longed to press her mouth to them, but before she could, Jess pushed her back down to the mattress.

"Not so fast." She grinned at Sadie. "I want to thank you properly for this special day." She lowered herself down and kissed Sadie's neck, nipping a trail from the sensitive skin behind her ear to her collarbone.

"You took me on the date, babe. I should be thanking you." Sadie moaned again as heat pooled between her legs. She traced her hands down Jess's back and slipped her fingers under the waistband of her boxers. "Also, keep doing that."

Jess continued the kisses and propped herself up on one elbow. She explored Sadie with her free hand, tracing the lines of the elaborate scroll of the treble clef tattoo on Sadie's hip with her fingertip, and then with a feather-light touch, she tickled her way back up to her breasts. Jess took one hard bud between her fingers and pinched it while she sucked the other one between her lips.

Sadie squirmed as she became wetter for Jess and her thong grew damp. She drew in a deep breath and her heartbeat pounded in her ears. "God, baby. You're driving me crazy." She bit out. "I need to feel you inside me."

Jess growled again and shifted her weight, sliding her hand from Sadie's breast straight down to the wet spot on her thong. She pawed at the lacy fabric while Sadie lifted her hips to help Jess access her heat. "I can't… I need to take this off you." She shifted again, this time onto her knees and tugged the offending thong over her hips.

"Wait." Sadie gasped. "Take yours off too."

An arch of an eyebrow was Jess's initial reaction, but then a grin broke across her face and she shook her hips while she pulled the briefs down until she was naked as well. "Is this what you wanted?" Her voice was thick and raspy and caused another delicious wave of tingles to surge through Sadie. Jess lowered herself back down to the bed and wasted no time finding Sadie's wetness with her palm.

Sadie moaned as she bucked her hips against Jess's pressure, moving in rhythm with her hand. At the same time she reached down and thrummed her fingers across Jess's swollen pussy. Jess let out a gasp and the resulting puff of air tickled at Sadie's neck and made her chest swell at her ability to elicit that response.

Sadie dipped her fingers into Jess's heat slowly at first, then with an increasing urgency. The heel of her palm rubbed at Jess's hardened clit with every thrust as she moved through her slickness, and her own excitement built.

"Don't stop." Jess sucked in her breath between words.

They moved together, pushing each other closer to the edge. Sadie slipped to that white space where thought and reason gave way to pleasure. As Jess cried out and her pussy clenched around Sadie's hand, Sadie crested and shook with the intense orgasm.

Jess rolled onto her back, put a hand on her chest, and gulped air as if to catch her breath. A satisfied smile appeared on her face as she reached her free hand over to grab Sadie's. She pulled her knuckles to her and tenderly kissed them.

Sadie propped herself up on her side, facing Jess. She let the silence stretch between them, enjoying the tangled web of their breathing. Jess's long eyelashes fluttered and a blissful expression bloomed on her face. Sadie's heart pounded inside her chest. It had been the perfect ending to the perfect date, and she hoped, the start of something even more wonderful for the two of them.

# CHAPTER FIFTEEN

Sadie stared blankly out the big windows at the front of Lenny's as she mindlessly wiped down the empty tables in her section Saturday evening. Even though Jess had left her house shortly after they had made love so that Sadie could get ready for work, she had remained on Sadie's mind for the entirety of her shift. Jess popped into her thoughts when she least expected them. Sadie didn't want to be stuck serving pizza and lite beer all night. She wanted to kiss Jess again. She wanted to do more than kiss her again. Mostly she wanted to prove to herself that it had all really happened in the first place.

She still couldn't believe that she had let her guard down for Jess—for anyone really. After all the crap Corey had put her through, she had picked up a fierce "I'll do me" attitude. She hadn't had any interest in getting back into the dating scene. She had only wanted to focus on the band. A lot of good that had done with the way Sugar Stix imploded before she left New York.

In spite of all that, when Jess kissed her in the alley after getting so worked up and jealous, the shell of fear around Sadie cracked and fell away. Jess's raw emotion—and the fact that she had been bold enough to express it out loud—had shattered Sadie's defenses. Their date had intensified things between them and now that she had let Jess in, Sadie didn't want to let her go.

"Hey, DuChamp." Michael's very annoying habit of calling her by her last name interrupted her thoughts. Did he even know her name was Sadie?

She glanced down at her wrist to check the time, forgetting her watch wasn't there. She had left it in Jess's room the night they had fallen in the pool and she still hadn't gone over to retrieve it. By her estimation she had looked at her bare wrist about a dozen times over the course of her shift. Old habits die hard. With a sigh she sauntered over to the bar where Michael was ticking inventory off on a clipboard. "What's up?"

"I got a lot of good feedback on you ladies the other night."

Pride swelled inside of her. It felt good to hear that people liked Regina Phalange. The ladies had worked hard to pull off that performance and they deserved all the kudos they received. "Great. Thanks, I'll be sure to let the rest of the band know."

"Any chance you want to do next Thursday too?"

The question caught her off guard. She had expected the gig at Lenny's would be a one-time thing. Everyone in the band *did* seem to enjoy it, though. She had no right to answer for the band without checking with the others first, but she did anyway. She would deal with the rest of Regina Phalange later. "Next Thursday? Hell, yeah."

The rest of her shift flew by with her brain trained on Regina Phalange's next gig, keeping those pesky, lustful Jess thoughts at bay, at least for the moment.

Friday and Saturday evenings in the summer usually meant one thing to Jess: Queen of Hearts events. Normally she didn't mind—a lot of times they were even fun—but for some reason the night was dragging. She suspected it had something to do with the fact that she would rather be spending her time with Sadie. But they both had to work, so Jess smiled and handed out Queen of Hearts key fobs and vodka samples despite the pinch in her toes from standing around in high heels all night.

When the action at the sample table eased up for a moment, she helped herself to one of the Black Licorice Jell-O shots. It was her favorite of the three flavors they were sampling that night. She let out a slow breath as the image of Sadie dripping wet after they fell into the pool the other night eased its way back into her mind. Sadie's dark hair slicked back, wet sports bra clinging to her… She was nothing short of sexy as fuck. When they got up to her room, it was all Jess could do to keep from throwing Sadie down on the bed and exploring every inch of her with her lips, devouring her. And then when she didn't think Sadie could get any sexier, she came out of the bedroom wearing Jess's clothes. That had been a total panty soaker for her. It was no wonder Jess couldn't keep her hands off Sadie on their date that afternoon. It was beginning to seem like she would never get enough of that woman.

"Hey, we're all out of Birthday Cake Jell-O shots." Shanna's whiny voice interrupted her reminiscing and brought her back to the moment and the task at hand. "Also, don't you think the name Black Licorice is redundant? That *is* licorice. The red stuff is cherry flavored and called Cherry Vines. It's not licorice. So there's no need to specify that licorice is black. The name of that vodka is all wrong."

Jess nodded with fake interest at Shanna's monologue and crossed her arms, afraid that her hard nipples were visible through her thin Queen of Hearts vodka tank top. Unfortunately, she wasn't quick enough to cover them up.

"Looks like someone's glad to see me." Shanna squeaked and giggled like she was the cleverest girl in the whole world. She slung an arm across Jess's shoulders and spoke against the skin on her neck. Her breath was so hot and sticky Jess wondered if it left a residue. "That's so sweet."

Jess shrugged and shook her off. "God, Shanna, what the hell has gotten into you lately?" Based on the strong licorice smell on Shanna, she guessed in that instant it was a hearty amount of the vodka they were handing out.

"Nothing. I'm trying to be friendly." Shanna pouted and linked an arm through Jess's elbow, clearly not getting the hint that Jess was not digging her handsy ways. "You never used to mind a little flirting before."

That wasn't exactly true. Jess had never exactly enjoyed Shanna's flirting; she merely tolerated and tried to ignore it. Despite her playgirl ways, Jess had never thought responding to Shanna's come-ons was a good idea since she was an employee of the family business. Plus after Jess's conversation with Sadie the day before about the subject, she really didn't want any blurred lines where Shanna was concerned. She usually managed to be a little more patient, but it seemed that patience had dried up right along with her fantasy about soaking wet Sadie. "Shanna, I'm trying to do my job here."

"We've been working together for what, four summers now?" Shanna's voice was as sickly sweet as the alcohol on her breath. "We've always had fun while on the job. We spend a shit ton of time together. Hell, we're practically like sisters."

"Okay, the sister thing makes the flirting thing even creepier." She shook her head.

"Joke, Jess. Take one." Shanna shrieked with laughter before sucking another Jell-O shot into her hot pink lipsticked mouth. She spun around and posed with one hand on her hip. Her face was still puckered and pouty and she rolled her eyes like a spoiled teenager. "Your sense of humor has completely gone missing as of late. Honestly, it's a total bummer."

"My sense of humor has not gone missing. I've had it with you hitting on me and pushing the boundaries of our professional relationship." Jess's ears burned hot. She couldn't make her stance on this any clearer. Between Shanna's crappy work ethic, her excessive drinking, and the annoying flirting that had given Sadie the wrong impression, Jess had finally had enough. "You and me are *never* gonna happen, Shanna, so please, *please* stop it with the flirting and the touching and the gauging of my sense of humor. It's none of your fucking business. We're coworkers, that's it. That's all it will ever be."

Shanna's jaw dropped and a look of hurt briefly flashed in her eyes, as if Jess had slapped her, but then just as quickly she recovered and fixed a smartass smirk on her face. "Coworkers, that's it. Sure thing." She shrugged and reached for yet another shot. "You got it, Ms. Moran."

Jess turned her back to Shanna, choosing to overlook the formal address. Too formal was better than too friendly in this case. She went back to arranging Queen of Hearts swag on the cocktail table. She would keep herself busy with her work, do her best to ignore Shanna, and get through the rest of the night. There was no sense in arguing with an inebriate anyway. She would train her brain back onto happy thoughts of the date she had with Sadie earlier and her plans for the next time they would be together.

# CHAPTER SIXTEEN

Sadie pulled into her driveway and stepped out of the car still singing the last song she heard on the radio. *No promises, no demands. Both of us knowing...love is a battlefield.* She had floated through the last bit of her shift at Lenny's daydreaming about pounding her drums in front of a crowd at another Regina Phalange gig and she was still buzzing with excitement about it.

The downstairs windows of the house glowed faintly with the light from the kitchen, but the upstairs level was completely dark. Her mom was probably already in bed but she'd left the lights on for her. Sadie glanced at her bare wrist to check the time yet again. Muscle memory was a powerful thing. A quick check of her phone showed it was barely past nine thirty—not exactly late night. She turned her gaze in the direction of the Morans' house, but the curve of the road kept the actual structure out of sight. Were lights glowing in the windows there? Jess wasn't home—she was working an event. But Marley could still be up. And Sadie was absolutely busting to share the news of Regina Phalange's invitation to another gig at Lenny's

Pizza. It wouldn't hurt to take a stroll down the street and see if Marley was around. Besides, Sadie needed to get her watch out of Jess's room anyway. The perfect excuse to drop by.

When she knocked on the Morans' door, Marley greeted her with her usual big bright smile. "Sadie, what are you doing here? Come on in." She pulled her robe tighter to cover up her pjs as she ushered Sadie into the house. "You know Jess isn't here though, right?"

"No, I know." Sadie stepped into the foyer as Marley shut the door behind her. She squinted at the light fixture shining on the ceiling. A moth had snuck in with her and was buzzing around the glass dome. "I…I left my watch here the other day and I thought I would grab it if you didn't mind. I think it's up in Jess's room."

"Oh, sure, honey." She waved a well-manicured hand toward the staircase. "Go on up. Help yourself."

Sadie thanked her over her shoulder as she took the stairs two at a time. She would grab the watch, and then before she left, she would ease into telling Marley the news about how she'd booked another gig for Regina Phalange without checking with the others.

The watch was right where she had left it on the dresser. She was heading back out to the hallway when she caught a glimpse of something on Jess's nightstand. It was that old photo of Jess and her mom. She stopped and picked it up, wanting to look at chubby, baby Jess again. She couldn't have been much older than one when it was taken. Her round cheeks smiled at the camera and her cute little baby hands were clapping together. She was totally sunshine and promise.

Sadie still couldn't get over Marley's old goth look. The dark hair really made a difference in her overall appearance. Her complexion was paler. Maybe she started tanning since then. Of course the picture had to be twenty years old, so there was bound to be some changes since then. Same big boobs though. Sadie was mentally scolding herself for even noticing her neighbor's boobs under the circumstances when Marley poked her head into the room, startling her enough that she actually jumped and stuck her hand with the photo in it behind her back. Busted.

"Hey, did you find it?"

"What?" Guilty heat filled Sadie's cheeks.

"Your watch. Did you find it?" Marley's cheerful voice indicated she was none the wiser about Sadie nosing around in Jess's personal belongings.

Sadie slipped the picture into the back pocket of her jeans so Marley wouldn't know she had been studying it. Jess had been very clear about how embarrassed her mom would be if someone saw her old style. There was no reason to do that to her, especially when she needed Marley to be in a good mood to receive the news about Regina Phalange. She would bring the photo back the next time she was at the Moran house. Nobody would be the wiser. "Oh, yeah. Thanks."

"Good." Marley led her back down the stairs. "Can I get you something to drink? I picked up some organic lemonade at the market today and it's delicious."

"Lemonade sounds great. Thank you." In the kitchen, Sadie hopped onto one of the tall chairs by the breakfast bar. She had really come to feel at home at the Moran house over the past couple of weeks since she had been back in Tucker Pointe. That was a good thing since she had the delicate task of announcing she had signed Regina Phalange on for another gig without consulting any of the others. The best way to break the news was probably swift and honestly—like pulling off a bandage. But a little flattery first couldn't hurt. "Michael said we were a big hit with customers at Lenny's last night. Everyone loved us. He was wowed."

"It was a lot of fun, wasn't it?" Marley set two glasses of lemonade with fresh lemon garnish to boot on the granite countertop. She climbed onto one of the empty chairs and tucked her fluffy robe around herself.

"I think the other women enjoyed themselves too." Sadie took a sip of her drink and smacked her lips against the tartness. The drink was sharp and refreshing after a long shift of waiting tables. "Even my mom, and that's saying something."

"Definitely more exciting than our usual clip-n-bitch coupon swap." Marley laughed and her eyes sparkled the same way Jess's did when she smiled. Like mother, like daughter.

"I'm glad you think so." Sadie took another gulp of lemonade before ripping off the bandage as planned. "Because I told him we would do it again next week."

Marley's mouth formed an O of surprise. "Regina Phalange playing at Lenny's again?"

"If we want to." She tried her best to give a casual shrug and look cool. She hoped Marley would give the response she wanted to hear, but she didn't want to pressure her. "Do we want to?"

"I think the others will want to." Marley's blond ponytail bobbed and bounced as she nodded, but something in her eyes indicated she wasn't completely on board. Her brow wrinkled as if she was making a mental pros and cons list.

"But you don't?"

"Sadie, honey, it's not that I don't want to." Marley sighed. "It's just that it's…complicated. I have a lot going on with the Queen of Hearts gala coming up, and Jess has been so worried about what gets put on the social media. She was pretty stressed out the last time we played Lenny's."

Heat creeped into Sadie's cheeks as visions of her and Jess packing up her drums mid-fight in front of everybody after the last Regina Phalange gig danced in her mind. She shook her head to clear it. They had worked that all out. Didn't Marley remember catching them making up—and making out—in the alley? Walking in on your daughter sucking face with the girl down the street didn't seem like the kind of thing that would slip one's mind. Marley also probably remembered Jess chasing Dan out of the alley after the show. "I guess she was a little high-strung that night."

"You know how Jess is. She worries about…" She puckered her lips like she was carefully monitoring which words slipped out. "It's been the two of us for a long time. She looks after her old mama."

"Old mama? Hardly." It was not a phrase Sadie would ever use to describe Marley. Sure, she was a mom, but as she sat there with her hair pulled back in a ponytail and one leg tucked under her on the stool, she barely looked a day over thirty. Sadie didn't know how old Marley was, but she had to have been fairly young when she had Jess. Marley was beautiful, smart, and fit. She could surely take care of herself. Anyway, playing a Regina Phalange gig wasn't anything dangerous. Jess was just being overly cautious at the last show. They would just stay away from Dan this time. That was no problem. Jess would be fine. It was time for Sadie to bring out the big guns and convince Marley to do it. "The thing is, I think the band has been really good for my mom. I've seen joy return to her eyes since we've started playing. It's still not a constant thing, but it's so much better than it has been. One more gig could be what it takes to push her past the finish line."

Marley nodded in agreement. "I know what you mean. I've seen a difference in her lately too. You've done a good job by her, Sadie." She reached across the counter and covered Sadie's hand with her own. "You're a good daughter."

To Sadie's surprise, her eyes welled with tears. She was doubtful that she could totally redeem herself for being neglectful when her mom needed her most, but it was still nice to get confirmation she was making steps in the right direction. She wiped her thumb under her eyes and forced a smile. "Thank you."

"Oh dear, don't cry." Marley squeezed her hand. "We'll play one more gig. You can tell Jennifer and I'll call Kristen and Sophie in the morning."

Relief washed over Sadie. She wasn't proud that she'd downplayed Jess's concerns to get Marley to agree to the gig, but one more show really could be what her mom needed to feel that joy again. Besides, it was a little odd that Jess was so overprotective of her mom. Both Jess and Marley said it was the result of their family being the two of them all these years. Maybe Sadie and her own mother's relationship would evolve into the same type of thing now that it was just the two of them in the house.

Her heart sank and her stomach felt like a burning chunk of coal had taken up residence in it. *Now that it was only the two of them in the house—without Dad.* The wide range in emotions she'd experienced over the course of her day was finally catching up with her. Suddenly she wanted nothing more than to be home tucked into her bed in the safe space of her childhood bedroom.

Her change in mood must have been evident in her face. Marley gave Sadie's fingers another gentle squeeze. "Hey, are you okay?"

Sadie scrubbed at her face with her free hand and exhaled loudly. "I'm sorry. I'm just tired. It was a long shift at work tonight."

It wasn't until Sadie was halfway down the street that she remembered the picture of Jess and her mom that was stashed in her pocket. She should have thought of some excuse to run back up to Jess's room to return it, but she didn't. Instead she had gotten freaked out thinking about leaving her mother home alone again and beat a hasty retreat. And now that she had, she couldn't exactly go back to return it. She would have to wait until morning, then find some excuse to drop by the Morans' house again. She would slip into Jess's bedroom and return the photo. And the problem would be solved. Easy peasy.

# CHAPTER SEVENTEEN

Jess rolled over in her bed and opened one sleepy eye, surprised to see sunlight already streaming through the slats of the blinds. She groaned and pulled the sheet over her face to block it out. She would need more sleep than that if she was going to function properly.

Her night had ended much later than she had intended. Not only had she packed up the Queen of Hearts stuff alone while a very drunk Shanna flirted with a bartender, she had also ended up giving Shanna a ride home afterward. As annoyed as she had been with her coworker, Jess had been worried that she was much too intoxicated to be put in the back of an Uber alone. The result of which was Jess not pulling into her own driveway until well after two in the morning. On top of that, her legs were still aching from doing it all in heels and there was a distinct pinch in her upper back she suspected was from helping a boozed, stumbling Shanna into her house. Chivalry sure came at a price.

The worst part was she hadn't even had a chance to talk to Sadie since their date the day before. They had exchanged a few texts while they were both at work but nothing meaningful enough to convey the feelings that had begun to flourish deep within Jess after their afternoon together in Sadie's bed.

Jess had been absolutely gobsmacked by the way her emotions had intensified while making love to Sadie. That had never been her experience with any woman before. There was something different—something special—between her and Sadie that she couldn't deny. It was more than a physical thing; it was as if Sadie saw straight into her soul when she looked into her eyes. Sadie had managed to knock down Jess's walls, and as much as Jess wanted to believe she was able to resist, deep down she knew she was putty in her hands. Jess had completely fallen for Sadie.

Closing her eyes she pulled up the mental image of kissing her way down Sadie's beautiful body, taking her time on the curve of her hip, and the moans her touch had elicited from Sadie. Immediately a lustful burn started in her core and her nipples went hard under her T-shirt. She slipped a hand down between her legs, but it only increased her frustration. She wanted more of Sadie, and the sooner the better. If she could drift off to sleep again maybe she could have her in her dreams. For the moment that would have to suffice.

But any thoughts she had entertained about returning to slumber were dashed though as a persistent plinky plunk of guitar strings coming from downstairs developed into full-on strumming, rousing her brain from that sweet, not-quite-awake space into reality. She threw the bedsheets off and grabbed her phone from her nightstand to check the time. 10:02 a.m. was not an unreasonable time in the morning for someone to be playing the guitar, but in Jess's still sleepy, achy-muscled mind it felt like a personal affront.

She rolled out of bed, pulled on gym shorts and a T-shirt she found on the floor, and tied her hair back into a ponytail. It wasn't a glamorous look, but it would do until she got some coffee and could think a little more clearly. She looked to her dresser for the photo of her and her mom to give it a morning ritual glance, but it wasn't there. It wasn't on the nightstand either. *Weird.* The fact that one of her most prized possessions had gone missing did nothing to improve her mood.

As she opened her bedroom door, her mother's singing and guitar playing wafted up. Jess recognized the tune—a soft, gentle ballad that paired beautifully with her mother's raw, raspy tone. It was the song Sadie had played for her at Lenny's on their date, and it would have brought tears to her eyes if she wasn't hell-bent on having a little peace and quiet after her late night out with Shanna.

She leaned heavily on the rail as she slumped her way down the stairs to the living room, where her mom was so lost in the music she didn't even notice her until the last notes of the song had faded into silence.

Her mother let out a gasp as she spotted her, then rested her guitar against the arm of the sofa. "Jess, you startled me."

"Sorry. I didn't want to interrupt you." She leaned against the wall and crossed her arms. "You're playing Sadie's song."

"Isn't it gorgeous?" Her mom's smile was dreamy and she placed a hand on her chest over her heart as if she was holding her emotions in place. She sighed and continued to gush. "It's beautiful, but I don't think Regina Phalange will be ready to play it at our gig at Lenny's next Thursday."

"Your gig next Thursday?" Jess's voice came out louder than she meant, but the statement caught her off guard. The gig at Lenny's was supposed to be a one-time thing, but her mother had definitely said *next* Thursday. "Regina Phalange is playing at Lenny's again? You promised you weren't going to keep doing this."

Her mother rose to her feet and put her hands on her hips. "Don't raise your voice at me. I promised you no such thing. And you're out of line speaking to me that way."

"I'm out of line?" Jess took a step closer. Her mom had said one gig would be it, and now she was totally going back on her word. Jess's tired head throbbed. "You're the one playing along with some teenage rock 'n' roll fantasy. We've worked so hard to bury the past behind us and now you're risking it all unravelling to play the guitar at some crappy pizza joint?

Seriously? Don't you get what people say on those other sites—how fast information is shared online? Aren't you worried about what this would mean for Queen of Hearts? What about that guy at Lenny's last time who followed you out of the bar? He totally recognized you."

"Jessica Rose, you better take a deep breath and remember who you are. Do I want my past brought into my present? No. I've worked really hard to leave that all behind. But I sell vodka, not Bibles, and I think that the alcohol-consuming public can get over it. When I started the company I worried about what would happen if people found out the truth, but I've built a brand and a product that is stronger than what I've overcome to get here. You're an adult now, and I don't have to worry anymore about you being the victim of cruelty from other kids. If people find out, so be it. I'm tired of hiding from the past." Her posture relaxed and her tone softened as she put a gentle hand on Jess's shoulder. "Honey, I know it's not going to be easy on either of us, but I'm ready to deal with the past. I just hope it doesn't change what my friends think about me."

*Deal with the past.* Those four little words should lift a gargantuan weight off Jess's shoulders, but as her mother's words buzzed in her mind, Jess found herself struggling to let the burden go. What would life be like without the constant struggle to contain the past? Her mom didn't seem unsure. She was taking the leap whether Jess was ready or not.

Her stomach went tight as if trying to hold on to the status quo, but Jess knew in her heart it was time. She blinked back tears and her throat fluttered as she breathed out the stress that had hummed in the background of her life for as long as she could remember. It felt weird and unnatural in a way, but also bright and fresh like a sunny summer morning after a stormy night. If her mom was ready to deal with the past, Jess would support her any way she could. Like she always did. Even if it did result in a marketing nightmare for Queen of Hearts. "Your friends will still think of you the same as always. Only with even more respect for all you've accomplished. They're good friends, don't sell them short. We'll come up with a plan to head off any backlash that Queen of Hearts gets when it all comes out. Let's just get through the twentieth anniversary gala without anyone finding out that you were—"

Her thought was cut short by the rapid pings of social media alerts on her phone. Glancing at the screen, her breath caught at the number of notifications indicating mentions of Queen of Hearts vodka. A couple quick clicks revealed brand-new accounts had been created across the various platforms for Regina Phalange.

Jess's stomach twisted uncomfortably as she pulled up the band's Facebook page to survey the content. There it was, the reason for the pings, a video of the Regina Phalange performance at Lenny's with hashtags and keywords to connect followers directly to the Queen of Hearts vodka sites. She watched a few beats of the video featuring her mom slinking across the stage dressed in all black. The hazy lighting of the bar gave the shot a very goth vibe. In fact, if she squinted her eyes at the shot she could definitely see her mom as....

"Oh, fuck, Sadie. How could you do this?" Stepping out of her mother's reach, she kicked her feet into the sport slides she'd left by the front door.

"Where are you going?"

"Out," she said simply as she yanked open the heavy front door and squinted against the bright sun.

"Jess, what is wrong? Come back and talk to me. Take a minute to calm down."

But the words barely registered in Jess's exhausted brain as she slammed the door behind her and marched down the street to the DuChamps' house. Every step pumped up her ire. Sadie convinced these women to start a band. Sadie talked them into playing at the party and got them not one, but two gigs at Lenny's. Sadie charmed Jess into letting her guard down. If she hadn't come back and stirred everything up, the neighborhood women would have continued on with their usual routine and her mother wouldn't be plastered all over social media looking like a gothed-up sex kitten.

Mrs. DuChamp was pulling out of the driveway as Jess made it to the bend in the street and the house came into view. Jess's footsteps quickened. Her heartbeat was pounding in her neck like it was building up to a total head explosion. She needed that video taken down, like, yesterday.

Fortunately, Jess only had to wait a few beats after knocking before Sadie opened the door.

"Hey you." Sadie looked carefree and genuinely happy to see her at first, but her expression dropped when Jess didn't return her high-wattage smile. "What's wrong?"

"What's wrong? What's wrong is you've got Regina Phalange all over social media."

"I've been waiting to surprise you in person. We got a second gig, so I thought we should promote ourselves a little. I thought you'd be happy for me—for us. Social media sites for Regina Phalange provides a little extra publicity for the show, and maybe some traffic for Queen of Hearts too."

"You've got to take that video down. Now."

Sadie's jaw dropped open and she stepped out of the doorway onto the front porch as she placed her balled fists firmly on her hips. Poised for battle. "You can't just march over here and demand I stop promoting my band. I'll post whatever I want on the Regina Phalange site."

"Like hell you will," Jess growled. "You are going to take it down and put an end to this…this…" Her sleepy brain grasped for words. "…madness."

"Seriously?" Sadie's voice slid up an octave and a half. "This madness? What happened to the supportive Jess who told me I was doing something special—that the neighborhood women had never seemed so happy? What's gotten into you?"

Jess bit her lower lip. She didn't have a good answer to give. She couldn't tell Sadie how dangerously close she was coming to exposing her mom's past without giving up the very secret they were trying so hard to bury. Around them the neighborhood was quiet except for the buzz of a lawnmower in the distance. The sun was shining cheerfully above them, indifferent to Jess's foul mood. Jess pushed at a strand of hair that had fallen loose from her bun, then rubbed the back of her neck.

It was hard to stay focused on her argument when Sadie looked so damn good in her black camisole and ripped-at-the-knee cargo shorts. It was true that she had done a complete turnaround from the things she had said to Sadie two days earlier, but she had to. She couldn't let her mother be exposed like this before the gala, and if destroying Regina Phalange was what it took to stop it, so be it. "This whole thing is ridiculous. You started a rock band with a bunch of middle-aged suburbanites. It's like you're hijacking their midlife crisis. You're using them to fill the long, boring hours while you're stuck here at home. To fill the year you promised your mom. You're being selfish."

Sadie's eyebrows shot up as shock registered on her face, but in a flash her eyes hardened with anger and her lips paled. Her hands slipped from her hips but remained balled in fists. Jess had taken it too far. "I'm not using anyone. Every woman in the group is having fun or else they wouldn't be doing this. Like you pointed out, they're middle-aged women. They can make up their own minds. They don't need you to do it for them. And the reason I started this band in the first place was because I was trying to take care of my mother, which is something I would think you would understand. But clearly you've got your head so far up your ass that you actually believe you're the boss of us all and can go dictating what we can or cannot do. God, Jess, I actually thought you were one of the good ones. I can't believe I fell for you."

The angry words stung, but Jess's stomach lurched at the tears in Sadie's eyes before Sadie closed the door with a slam. Jess stood and stared at the DuChamps' front door, silently willing Sadie to come back out—even if it was only to fight about Regina Phalange a little more—but no movement came from inside the house. It was over.

A cloud passed in front of the sun casting a darkness across her as if to point out it was time for her to retreat. Her shoulders slumped as she turned to head home. All she'd set out to do was protect her mom's business and spare herself a social media shit storm, but her relationship with Sadie had become collateral damage.

Slamming the front door behind her, Sadie marched up the stairs and fell onto her bed. She grabbed the big bunny Jess had won for her at the carnival, and wrapped her arms around it. In her heart she knew Jess was right. Regina Phalange was a band made up of middle-aged housewives who weren't serious about music, and occasional gigs at Lenny's was really as far as it was going to go. But something about being in front of a crowd made Sadie crave more and more of it. She got swept up in the excitement. Maybe what she was really angry about was that Jess had hit the nail on the head—she couldn't survive the year in Tucker Pointe without performing, and that scared the hell out of her. She needed music as much as she needed air to breathe. Maybe she really was clinging to Regina Phalange for her own sake as much as her mother's. She shouldn't have gotten so angry with her, but the way Jess had appeared on her doorstep demanding she take down the Regina Phalange social media posts had pushed all of Sadie's buttons.

What would she do once the gigs at Lenny's dried up? Her heart was heavy in her chest. Without her music, she would wither and die. With no performances to look forward to everything around her just seemed gray. Regina Phalange was filling that void for now, but how long would that last, and how could she keep her promise to her mom to stay with her in Tucker Pointe for a year without something to satisfy her need to rock out on stage? She was a terrible daughter, and she had just slammed the door in the face of the only person she wanted to talk it over with.

She rolled over and pulled out the drawer on her nightstand, rummaging blindly through it until she felt the tattered edge of the photo in her hand. She looked at smiling baby Jess again, and as usual, she smiled back. *God, she was a cute baby*. She really needed to return the photo to Jess's bedroom. She also needed to work off the stress that had gathered in her shoulders since she had argued with her. Fortunately she had a cure for that.

Picture still in hand, Sadie bounded down the steps to the living room, parked her butt on the stool at her drum set, and tucked the corner of the pic into the lip of the small tom. She picked up her sticks and twirled them between her fingers for a moment, while her mind slid down her mental playlist to find the perfect song. She settled on a Sugar Stix original she had written, "Bird In The Hand," and went to it, pounding out her frustration. Soon she was lost in the music, the bliss of the beat.

It wasn't until the last cymbal crash simmered down that she heard the doorbell. It was being pressed over and over in rapid succession, dinging incessantly.

"Okay! I hear you!" Sadie yelled as she rose from the stool and hustled to the front door. It had to be Jess coming back either to apologize or for round two of whatever the hell had gotten into her that morning. Sadie hoped it was the former. She was in no mood to entertain further discussion about Regina Phalange. The bell rang three more times. What kind of jerk reacted that way when someone failed to answer the door?

As she yanked the door open, a scowl already plastered firmly on her face, she got the obvious answer. Standing with a finger still pointed at the ringer was the last person on earth she expected to see—her ex from New York, Corey.

"What the hell are you doing here?"

"Sadie." He lowered his bell-ringing finger and flashed a grin that would be charming if it were on someone else instead of his pale, gaunt face. "Is that any way to greet an old lover?"

"God, you're so dramatic." She sighed and crossed her arms, while he leaned his lanky body against the doorjamb. Whatever power he once had over her was long gone. "What do you want, Corey?"

"Well, that's direct." He looked taken aback as if the horrible past they shared had never happened and she had no reason to be defensive around him, as if the strung-out nights, the verbal abuse and the violence had been expunged from his memory. "Aren't you going to invite me in?"

"I wasn't planning on it." Over his shoulder she could see his beat-up pickup truck parked on the street.

He stared at her intently, as if he were waiting for her to say more, or at least that she was joking, but she held her ground. Finally he cleared his throat, blinked hard a few times, and tried again. "I was hoping you would talk to me. Let me apologize."

Sadie stood firm. "I'm listening."

His gaze flicked over her shoulder to the living room, then down to his feet. He plucked his thumb against the seam of his jeans with one hand, and shoved the other into his front pocket. "Do you think we could do this inside?"

"No, I don't think so."

"Please." He finally looked her in the eye again, and she caught a glimpse of something she had never seen before in his face—remorse. "I'm sober now. I want to make things up to you."

Sadie looked him over from head to toe. Same ripped-up dirty jeans, same old eighties heavy metal band T-shirt, same shaggy cut, dirty blond hair. But there was something different too. His eyes weren't bloodshot and shifty like they used to be, and he appeared to be steady on his feet, which he almost never was toward the end of their relationship. Thinking his sudden appearance on her doorstep could be part of a twelve-step thing, she softened. She would never give him a second chance as a boyfriend, but she could give him a second chance to act like a decent human. She stepped aside to let him in. "Okay. But fifteen minutes. That's it. And if you push it even the teensiest bit, I'm calling the cops. No ifs, ands, or buts."

He stepped into the house, now both hands in pockets, but waited for her to lead the way to the couch. She sat first, but after he plopped down comfortably beside her, she scooted a little more in the opposite direction. Giving him the chance to apologize was one thing, letting her guard completely down was a whole other subject. She would not tolerate any type of physical contact, raised voice, or violent language. She had her walls up, and this time they would not crumble. She had left New York about a month before, and they had broken up only a few months before that. But less than six months sober was still better than none.

"So, you drove here from New York to apologize to me? That's an awfully long drive."

He nodded and wrung his hands in his lap. Nervous. But not his old paranoid kind of nervous. This seemed to come from a more genuine place. "I scared you, and I hurt you, and I generally treated you like crap when we were together, and I'm very sorry. You didn't deserve that. Nobody deserves that, and I know it. I'm different now that I'm off the trash. I realize I've made a lot of mistakes. I've hurt a whole lot of people, and I regret that, especially what I did to you. But I'm trying to make a fresh start."

"Good, Corey." She nodded encouragingly, glad he was getting the apology off his chest, and touched that he had bothered to do it at all. "I'm really happy for you making that change. I'm sure it hasn't been easy."

"No, it hasn't. But there was another reason I came to see you." He stopped and picked at the loose wispy white strings of the denim surrounding the hole at his knee. Sadie winced but didn't comment on the way he carelessly dropped them onto the rug. Apparently his slobbish tendencies were not one of the changes he had made since they broke up.

Sadie closed her eyes, wanting to block out whatever words were going to come out of him next. If it was anything about them getting back together, she was totally prepared to drag him right back out of the house by his earlobe. "Yeah?"

"Yeah. I've been focusing on my music a lot recently, and I'm getting a band together. We could really use a drummer, and when I heard Sugar Stix broke up, I figured you might be available. You interested in getting back in the scene?"

Her eyes flew open, but Corey didn't seemed to be alarmed by that. He sat there calmly, his gaze fixed on her, waiting for her answer. He was asking her to join a band—a band that would potentially have gigs in New York City. She could be part of the nightlife she missed so much—the rush of performing, the energy of the crowd. *Damn.* Working with the old Corey would have sucked, but the new, level-headed Corey might be okay as a bandmate. As long as he didn't relapse. A real band in New York!

*In New York.*

She glanced over at the stack of unread newspapers and unopened mail that had remained on the dining room table since her mother's last effort at tackling it. She had spotted an issue of *O* magazine from five months prior sticking out of the bottom of the pile earlier that day. Things that previously her mother had always remained on top of. Before her father died. Before she was alone. Sadie's stomach twisted. Mom still wasn't back to her normal self. There was no way she could leave her yet. She had to stay in Tucker Pointe. She'd made a promise. What kind of crappy daughter did it make her that she was even considering it? Mom clearly still needed her at home.

"Sadie?" Corey shifted on the couch beside her and she flinched and changed positions too, in case he was trying to slide closer to her. "What do you think?"

"Um." She chewed her bottom lip. There was no need to burden Corey with the truth about the situation. They weren't even friends, really. Hell, they had still been a couple when her father had passed away, and Corey hadn't even been all that sympathetic about it then. He could never understand what she was going through with her mom, whether he was getting clean for real or not. "I appreciate the offer, and I'm really happy for you, but I can't do it. I have a thing going here. I'm already involved with a band, and we have gigs lined up that I can't bail on." *Well, one gig. Whatever.* It was tiny stretch of the truth. Soon Corey would be on his way and it wouldn't matter what she had said to him anyhow.

"You've got a band? Here?" Corey's posture straightened and as he stretched his back making him taller in his seat. It was as if he was taken aback by her statement.

"It's a little thing, but it keeps me busy." She shook her head determined not to sell Regina Phalange short like that. They were a hell of a lot more than a *little thing*. Those women were coming through for her and her mom. They deserved better than that. "It's actually going really well. We're an all chicks band and we've got an edgy sound."

"Sadie DuChamp and Her All Chicks Rock 'N' Roll Band. I like the sound of that." Corey stood and scratched at his stubbly chin as he meandered over to the drum set in the corner of the living room. "I'm on my way to pick up a buddy in Milwaukee now, and then we're coming through here on our return to

New York. Are you playing anywhere that we could catch you in action? I'd love to get an eyeful of this." He ran a finger along the rim of the snare.

An eyeful of the all chicks band. Sure he would. But he should see with his own eyes the proof that Sadie was doing fine without him. She shrugged. "Well, yeah. The band is actually called Regina Phalange. We're playing at Lenny's Pizza here in Tucker Pointe next Thursday. It's a small place, but we're doing a set. I can text you the details."

"Sounds great." Corey's distracted tone drew her attention to what he was doing. His eyes were locked on the photo of Jess and Marley. "Why do you have a picture of Rikki Snow on your drums? You change teams again or something?"

Sadie ignored his inquiry regarding her sexual identity. It certainly wasn't any of his business. "Who?"

"Rikki Snow, nineties porn star? Her flicks still fly off the shelves at our store. I get why, she's hot as fuck. This bitch here." A hint of the old Corey was back in his voice as he held the photo out in front of him. Apparently he was still holding down his job at the adult bookstore. At least he'd managed to keep a job. Sadie strode over and plucked it right from his fingers, protective of Jess's personal item and irritated that he had referred to Marley as a bitch.

"That's not a porn star. That's my girlfriend's mom." It was the first time she had referred to Jess as her girlfriend out loud, or at all really, but in that moment of standing up for her and her family, it felt right. Whatever had happened between them earlier had been a mistake. Some kind of miscommunication. She needed to talk to Jess and work it out. But first she had to get Corey the hell out of her house and on his way. "She's definitely not whoever you think she is."

Corey scrunched his face up, like she had gone mad. "Girlfriend? So you did switch teams. Good on ya. Anyway, the story goes, Rikki Snow was murdered by some psycho twenty-something years ago. Creepy stuff. But there are fans who believe she's not really dead, that the production company just put that story out there for some kind of legal mumbo jumbo cover their ass reason. And now you're telling me this picture is your girlfriend's mom who is alive and well but looks just like her? It *could* be a weird coincidence, I guess."

"Okay, Corey. Your fifteen minutes are up. Time to hit the road." Sadie was out of patience with the reunion. She'd heard enough of his nonsense. She grabbed Corey by the upper arm and pulled him through the living room to the front door. "Thanks for stopping by."

He tripped over his own feet as she dragged him along, but before she managed to actually shove him outside, he turned to face her one last time. "Are you *sure* you don't want to drum for us? It could be a lot of fun."

Sadie rolled her eyes at his whiny tone. Always total drama with Corey. That hadn't changed either. "I'll text you with the details of the set at Lenny's. Congrats on the sober thing. That's really great." She watched him mosey halfway down the front walk before shutting the door, locking it for good measure, and leaning her back against it. When she finally heard his truck start up and noisily drive off with its rusty death rattle, she blew out the breath she had been holding and looked at the photograph still in her hand. The unexpected visit from her ex had shaken her, but at least she knew two things for sure. She had to find out what the hell had Jess so out of sorts earlier, and she had to get the picture back in Jess's room before she noticed it was missing.

# CHAPTER EIGHTEEN

Jess had returned home from the DuChamps' house, stomped down to the basement, and parked herself in front of the TV for some mindless, stress-relieving video games. Everything good she had built with Sadie had been blown to hell because of fucking secrets. It started out as something her mother was protecting her from, but as time went by, those roles had somehow shifted until Jess had become the protector. Maybe her mom was right and Jess had taken all this social media stuff too seriously. Maybe there were some things that were just out of their control.

Controlling her mother's secrets had never affected Jess's romantic life in the past. She made sure of it by never allowing herself to get that involved with anyone. She always moved on to the next girl before things got serious and she had to tell the lover about her mother, the porn star. Jess had known the truth herself since she was a senior in high school. Her mom had sat her down and explained it all to her, not wanting her to find out some other way when she left home for college. Best it came straight from the source, she'd said. Jess had struggled with the information at first, but realized eventually that nothing she'd learned changed who she knew her mother to be. She'd accepted it as the past and dealt with keeping the secret. But then along came Sadie. Suddenly Jess had another feeling strong enough to challenge her need to control.

On the television screen Pac-Man chomped through the maze, avoiding the ghosts and collecting fruit in his easy-peasy digital life. In Jess's mind, nothing seemed so clear cut. Her stomach had a sick, queasy, upside down feeling, and her scalp was prickling with guilt. Those secrets she had swallowed down had twisted into anger, and she had taken that out on Sadie, when really Sadie wasn't to blame at all.

Then there was that other strange feeling—the one lumped in a ball in her throat. The one that whispered she had broken something precious, the one that was bringing tears to her eyes.

She vividly recalled Sadie's words before she slammed the door. *I fell for you.* Sadie felt the same way she did—at least until that morning when Jess fucked everything up. She dropped the game controller onto the couch beside her and blew out a deep breath. Her heart sunk. Maybe there was still a way to fix things. She blinked dumbly at the screen as Pac-Man was gobbled up by the ghosts surrounding him, not an encouraging sign.

But explaining herself to Sadie required giving up a secret that wasn't Jess's to tell. She couldn't betray her mother, but she couldn't be in a relationship with Sadie and continue to hide things from her. They would end up having the same fight over and over again, like Sadie had said, until it finally destroyed them.

She was in love with Sadie DuChamp, and unless she could make things right, she would be living with this ache in her heart for a long, long time.

Her eyes stung and she sucked her lip between her teeth as the tears began to roll down her cheeks. She hugged her knees to her chest in an act of self-comfort. Her whole body shook as she tipped her head down in defeat.

"Jess, honey, what happened?" Her mother's gentle voice from the basement stairs let her know she was no longer alone.

Jess quickly rubbed her fists against her teary eyes. "Nothing. I'm fine." She lied and stretched the length of the couch. She felt bad enough about struggling to keep their secret from Sadie; she didn't need to put that guilt on her mother as well.

"Don't *I'm fine* me. I know you better than that." Her mother's voice was light as she plopped down next to Jess on the couch and pulled her into her arms. "You went storming off to Sadie's like a bat out of hell, then came home and stomped directly to the basement where you holed yourself up for over an hour until I finally found you down here sobbing on the couch. You're not fine."

"No, I'm not," Jess confessed, and to her surprise, a fresh wave of tears spilled over. "I lost my temper and said some things to Sadie—really horrible things—and I hurt her. She'll probably never speak to me again. I've ruined everything." The words bubbled over much like her tears—hard to stop once they started.

"Oh, Jess." She cradled her daughter and ran her hand through her hair. It was the kind of comfort you could only get from a mom. "I'm sure it's not that bad. Sadie's a reasonable person. You need to apologize. This will blow over. You'll see. You really like her, huh?"

"I think I'm in love with her." Jess couldn't help smiling at the look of shock that crossed her mother's face. She sniffed and swiped her thumb at the last of the tears on her face, then hugged a throw pillow to her chest—a small barrier to her exposed feelings. "I know, I know. It's weird, but I've never felt this way with any other girl. There's something special about her."

"Something special." Her mother repeated with a nod and her smile reached her eyes and lit up her whole face. "Then what are you doing sitting down here playing video games? Go tell her how you feel. Go get her back."

Jess squeezed her eyes shut and shook her head. Telling Sadie how she felt was much easier said than done. "It's not that easy. I can't…I can't let her in. It's too complicated."

Her mom pulled back in surprise, her features scrunched up in confusion. "What's too complicated—you and Sadie? Because you're going back to school at the end of summer?"

Jess pushed herself against the cushions on the couch, burrowing in. She didn't want to hurt her mother's feelings, but she was too raw from the emotional morning to be anything other than truthful. "Not school, Mom. Us. Me, you, the past. I can't be with Sadie if I can't be honest with her."

"Oh, baby." Tears shone in her mother's eyes. "I never meant for you to have to make a choice like that. You deserve all the love and happiness you can find in this world. I don't want you to miss out on a single thing life has to offer. Neither of us should have to close ourselves off from joy because of fear." She reached across the cushion and took Jess's hand in hers. "That's what I was trying to tell you this morning. When I started singing with Regina Phalange I felt a joy I hadn't experienced in a long time. And it felt *damn good*. It's what made me see that I'm going to have to deal with the past if I want to really live. If that's how Sadie makes your heart feel, then you should go for it. Like I said before, it's time for me to deal with the past."

"Mom, aren't you worried that—"

"Stop. We can have that joy if we want to. If you're in love with Sadie, you have to be able to trust her. If you think that she's special, that's good enough for me. Now, go wash your face. Go tell Sadie the truth. Tell her how you feel about her."

Jess hesitated a brief moment before hopping up from the couch and tossing the pillow she'd been holding to the floor. She paused to kiss her mom on the top of the head before making a dash for the stairs. "Thanks, Mom!"

# CHAPTER NINETEEN

Sadie patted the deep cargo pocket of her shorts where the photo of baby Jess was safely tucked, and strode down the street to the Morans' house.

Since her talk with Corey, her whole perspective had turned around. The moment the word *girlfriend* had slipped through her lips, everything had changed in her mind. She and Jess had something real—something worth fighting for. When you cared about someone you got to the root of the problem and worked things out. There was no way that Jess was honestly that bent out of shape about a gig at Lenny's Pizza. There had to be some underlying reason that she was so upset, and like a good girlfriend, Sadie was going to talk it over with her, *really* listen, and help her through it.

And return that photograph while she was at it.

Although she had been flattered by Corey's offer to join his band, her excitement had waned once he drove away and reality set in. Inviting him to the Regina Phalange gig was probably a bad idea. Corey may have said he'd changed, and he did appear sober and sincere when he stopped by, but it was hard to ignore a year's worth of memories that advised she proceed with caution whenever he was around. For all she knew, he might not even be back with this friend from Milwaukee. Hell, for all she knew, the friend might not even exist at all. She should've sent him on his way and been done with it.

Sadie swallowed her regret about Corey and reached out to poke her finger at the doorbell of the Morans' house when Jess yanked the front door open.

Both girls gasped and then spoke at the same time.

"We need to talk."

"I was just coming to see you."

Jess stepped backward into the house, rubbed the back of her neck, and smiled sheepishly. "You're right. We need to talk. Come in."

"You were coming to see me?" Sadie kicked her flip-flops off while Jess closed the door behind her. Marley was singing in the kitchen and from the smell of it, baking something sweet.

"Yeah. I wanted to apologize." Jess seemed momentarily distracted as she looked from the dining room to the living room. "Let's go up to my room. We'll have privacy there."

Sadie nodded enthusiastically. Jess's bedroom was perfect. They could talk things out, and then she could return the photo, nice and easy. "Lead the way."

Once upstairs, she made herself comfortable on the corner of Jess's queen-size bed, but Jess paced the room after she shut the door. Her gym shorts and T-shirt looked less than fresh and her hair was pulled back haphazardly in a ponytail, but in Sadie's eyes she was perfectly beautiful. She was her girl. "Come on. Sit down next to me."

Jess tucked one leg under her as she sat, so she was facing Sadie when she spoke. "I owe you an apology for the way I acted this morning. I'm so sorry I hurt you. I should have never said those awful things; there's…there's no excuse for that." She rubbed her fist at her teary eyes and shook her head. When she spoke again, her voice was quieter. "I haven't been completely honest with you. I need to explain why I reacted the way I did. It's time I let you in."

"You don't have to tell me anything."

Jess scrubbed at her face with her hands and pulled in a deep breath. "Yes I do have to tell you because I don't want to lose you. Sadie, I want us. I know I've been weird, and I at least owe you an explanation."

Sadie reached out and took Jess's hand in her own, pulling it down to expose her whole face. Brushing her thumb across her knuckles, she silently telegraphed encouragement for Jess to have her say. *Jess wanted them.* She wanted the relationship like Sadie did. If patience was what she needed, Sadie would deliver.

Blowing out a big breath, Jess began. "My mom lost both her parents in a car accident when she was eight years old. She grew up in the foster care system, bounced from one house to the next. The minute she turned eighteen she took off for California with hopes of being an actress and never looked back. I guess it was a very nineties thing to do." She paused and rubbed at her forehead like she was trying to scrub her stress away. Based on the creases that remained when her hands pulled away, it hadn't worked. "But once out in La La Land she didn't get an acting gig, she got pregnant. With me. She and her boyfriend got a tiny apartment and she waited tables at the restaurant where he was a cook, and they scraped by, but it was tough. After she had me, he talked her into doing porn for the fast cash. He knew a guy, and it was big money back then. Please don't judge her—I never have. She did what she had to do to survive."

"I would never." Sadie shook her head. It was a shock to hear, but she knew how hard it could be when you were chasing your dreams and you'd do anything to reach them. She was in no place to judge anyone's choices. Slowly the pieces of Jess's story clicked into place. Corey had been right about the woman in the picture. "Your mom was Rikki Snow?"

Jess chewed on her bottom lip and nodded. Acknowledging the truth without saying the words out loud.

"But Rikki Snow is dead."

She nodded again. "That's where the story really gets dark."

*Darker than your mom doing porn to survive?* Sadie held that thought in and let Jess continue.

"My father was...well, he wasn't really a great guy. He had a bad temper. He'd been rough with her before, but after she had me it got worse. One day they were fighting about money right before she left to go to work. He thought she was holding out on him. He followed her to the set and beat her pretty bad." Jess's voice had slid down to a whisper, but Sadie hung on every word. "A security guard from the set heard them and broke it up, but when my father rounded on him, the guard shot him. He killed him. I was two."

"Oh my God, Jess. I'm so sorry. I had no idea." The bedsprings squeaked as Sadie shifted to put an arm around Jess's shoulders.

"Of course you didn't." Jess waved a hand in the air, banishing the apology before swiping at the tears on her cheeks.

"All because your father thought your mom was hiding money from him."

"Well, she was." She shrugged and a whisper of pride flashed across her face. "She'd been saving up to take me and leave his abusive ass. Anyway, the production company didn't want any more trouble and agreed to let her out of her contract. They started the rumor that Rikki Snow had died in the incident on set that day too. Thank God it was the late nineties and there was no social media like now. Hell, people barely used the Internet then. Plus there weren't any records of Rikki Snow really existing—it was only a stage name. My mom used the money to move us to Chicago, reinvent herself, and start Queen of Hearts. The rest is history."

Sadie felt like her jaw was on the floor. Marley had been through so much. It made her success in business shine even brighter in Sadie's eyes. "That is incredible. All this time I never knew."

"Like I said, no one did. And Mom's worked damn hard to keep it that way. So have I. But those Rikki Snow fans are relentless. They pop up every couple years with conspiracy theories and speculation that Rikki Snow isn't really dead at all. Most likely because someone catches a glimpse of Mom somewhere. Times like that keeping an eye on the social media sites can be a real nightmare. You should see some of the things people post." A hint of a smile returned to Jess's face. "That's why she doesn't like to do the promotional events for Queen of Hearts herself. She tries to lay low. It's been over twenty years, but my mom still worries she'll be outed as her alter ego and it will change what people think of her or her company. Not to mention she'd have to deal with those fanatics harassing her. Porn fans can be awfully possessive of their favorites."

A thought settled over Sadie. "That's why you weren't exactly thrilled with our band playing at Lenny's. You were afraid someone would recognize her. You really were protecting her."

"Yes. I was only doing what I'd promised her to do from the start." She gave Sadie's hand a squeeze. "I'm sorry I was such a dick about it."

Her apology made Sadie smile in spite of herself. Knowing the motive behind Jess's behavior made it much less dickish and much sweeter. "It was understandable with the situation."

"But Sadie," Jess shifted again so she could look her straight on, "please don't tell anyone any of this. She's fought so hard to bury Rikki Snow in the past. But it's her story, and she'll tell people when she's ready."

Sadie met Jess's gaze. "You can trust me. And, babe, I'm sorry too." She put a hand on her shoulder and gave it a tender squeeze. Jess's defined arm muscles popped and twitched under her touch. "I knew there was something bothering you—something wrong—and instead of being a good girlfriend I—"

Jess's eyes went wide with surprise as she grabbed at Sadie's hand on her shoulder. "Did you say *girlfriend?*"

"Oh. No. I mean, yes." Her mind raced. Of course they hadn't actually discussed the status of their relationship. She had blurted it out assuming that girlfriends were what they were. Possibly a completely different perspective than how Jess saw the two of them. "Yes, I did say *girlfriend*, but I didn't mean—"

Marley's voice from downstairs interrupted her. "Girls, I'm running to the store. Listen for the timer on the oven for me, okay?"

"You got it, Mom!" Turning her full attention to Sadie, she lowered her voice. "You want to be my girlfriend?" She intertwined her fingers with Sadie's and moved their hands to her lap. In spite of the tear rolling down her cheek, her expression brightened. Jess wasn't put off by Sadie calling her girlfriend. She was happy.

Sadie's pulse quickened and she swallowed against the lump in her throat. "Yes, I do."

Jess leaned in closer at Sadie's response to her question. Her chest swelled and heat rushed up her neck. After everything that happened between them, after the way she had acted earlier that morning, Sadie still wanted to be her girlfriend. She focused her eyes on Sadie's dark, cherry-lined lips. They were plump and shiny like a sweet, juicy treat. She wondered if they tasted like candy. "The feeling is very, very mutual."

"Girlfriends it is then." Sadie's candy-coated lips let the words slip between them right before they made contact, pressing firmly against Jess's. Her hand slid fully into her hair and around to the back of her neck, holding her in close.

Jess responded immediately, slipping one hand up the leg of Sadie's cargo shorts, digging what little nails she had into the smooth flesh of her thigh. Her tongue traced her girlfriend's lips before probing and parting them. Sadie hungrily took her in, moaning softly as she sucked on her.

The sound of Sadie's sweet moans did Jess in and heat pooled between her legs. She gasped as Sadie broke off the kiss and moved seamlessly down to her neck, first giving her pop kisses, then landing her mouth on Jess's clavicle, teasing it with her tongue. Sadie's other hand slipped under the edge of her T-shirt and played lightly across her abdomen. Inhaling sharply, she felt her nipples tighten, and she longed for Sadie to put her hands on them. The anticipation was divine.

Jess stood up and pulled Sadie to her feet as well. She grabbed on to Sadie's tank top and pulled it up over her head, letting it fall to the floor. Jess wasn't surprised to find Sadie hadn't been wearing a bra; her breasts were not huge, but they were perky and magnificently round. She couldn't help but put her mouth right to them, flicking her tongue over one nipple, then moving to the other. She settled on sucking on the left one as she helped Sadie shimmy out of her shorts and thong.

Sadie reached down to tug Jess's gym shorts off her hips. Jess hadn't bothered to put on panties when she rolled out of bed that morning, and as her shorts hit her ankles, she felt Sadie's hand drag lazily over her pussy, giving her shivers that ran the length of her body.

When the last of their clothes had been tossed aside, Jess backed Sadie against the wall. She placed a hand on each side of Sadie and leaned forward to kiss her, gently biting her lower lip. In response Sadie hitched a leg up on Jess's hip, opening herself to her. Jess's breath caught as her girlfriend's fingers slipped into her wetness, separating her swollen, pulsing heat. She slid a hand down to explore Sadie as well.

"Mmmmm," Sadie murmured against her cheek when they broke the kiss. "Babe, I want you so bad."

She didn't need to ask twice.

Jess kissed her once again, then spun her off the wall and pushed her down onto the bed. She began to work her way down Sadie's body, encouraged by the sexy sound of her soft moans. She teased her for a moment by kissing her thighs, then sucking on one hard enough to leave a purple mark, before going after her open slit. She ran her tongue along the delicate ridge of her lips, then one long, slow stroke over the whole warm, wet opening.

Sadie cried out and Jess knew exactly what she was longing for. She circled Sadie's clit with her tongue a few times before sucking it gently between her teeth and sliding two fingers into her. She thrust in and out slowly and evenly while keeping pressure on Sadie's swollen pearl.

"Oh my god, Jess." Sadie gasped. "Fuck me!"

At the sound of her name, Jess increased her pace, slamming her fingers deeper into Sadie, and pressing her tongue firmly against Sadie's clit until she finally felt her body squeezing her fingers. While Sadie screamed out with pleasure, Jess continued to press deep for a beat and the warm rush of Sadie's juices soaked her hand. Her own body gave a shudder, pleased that she had so completely satisfied her girlfriend. She collapsed on the bed beside Sadie, wrapped her arms around her, and took deep breaths to calm her racing heart.

Sadie exhaled against Jess's chest, content with their naked bodies warm and pressed together. She basked in the blissful afterglow of their passion as Jess kissed her tenderly on the forehead and held her tight in her strong arms.

"You all right, rock star?" Her voice was soft and gentle and Sadie grinned at how that nickname had evolved into a term of endearment.

"I'm more than all right." Sadie's words came out raspy and thick. Her breathing was still easing to its normal pace.

"You need a drink, babe? I'll get us some water. I need to run down and check on the muffins in the oven anyway."

She didn't want to untangle their bodies, but if Jess left the room to get them drinks, it would present the perfect opportunity to return the picture of her and her mom. The last piece of the puzzle that would make everything right between them. "Yes please."

Jess slid out of bed and pulled her T-shirt and shorts back on. Sadie waited until she heard footsteps on the stairs before making a move. She didn't bother to dress. With any luck she would be back in the sheets like nothing had happened in no time at all. She rushed over to her cargo shorts and dug her hand in a pocket—the photo was there somewhere—but she came up empty. She flipped the shorts and desperately jabbed her hand into the pocket on the other side. Finally, she had the picture in her grasp. She was going to pull off the return, no problem.

Until she realized the charm on her necklace was snagged on a thread on the seam of the shorts. She had to get out of it quick before Jess got back upstairs. Her heart jumped to her throat. She was running out of time. If she yanked at the thread she ran the risk of breaking her necklace, and she really wanted to avoid that. On the other hand, she didn't want Jess to find her in that compromising position. Nobody looked sexy with a pair of shorts tethered to their neck.

She took a deep breath, pinched the charm between her fingers, and with the other hand, wiggled the thread until it popped out from where it was trapped. *Success!* She grabbed at the floor where she had dropped the photograph, and stood up to return it to Jess's dresser when she realized Jess was already standing in the doorway, two bottles of water in her hands, leaning against the jamb and studying her.

*Busted.*

"What's going on?" At first her expression was amused, the hint of a grin playing at the corners of her big, sexy mouth. But when her gaze landed on the tattered photo in Sadie's hand, something shifted in her eyes—a glaze of cool hardness set in. "Is that the picture of me and Mom? Where did you find it? I've been looking for it."

"Um. Yeah. I just...." Sadie stammered as hot guilt rushed up her neck into her face betraying her shame at taking the picture from Jess's room in the first place. "I was returning it."

"What the hell, Sadie? You took it?"

"It's not like that." She protested, suddenly very aware that arguing with someone while butt naked was way less comfortable than...pretty much anything else. "I was looking at it again the other day when I was here, and your mom came in the room, so I stuck it in my pocket so she wouldn't know I'd seen it."

"So you took it." Her voice was hard as the look of steel in her eyes.

"I didn't mean to." Sadie's thin excuse sounded feeble even to her own ears.

"Give it to me." Jess held out her hand and stared down at the floor, obviously not wanting to look at Sadie and her naked awkwardness. "Give. It. To. Me."

Tears welled in Sadie's eyes as she placed the photo in her open hand. The difference between the smiling, baby Jess in the picture and the hurt, angry Jess in front of her was both striking and heartbreaking. She hadn't meant to upset Jess. If only she had the chance to explain. It was a mistake to take the photo in the first place and she knew it was wrong, but she was trying to spare Marley's feelings like Jess had asked her to. She sniffed to hold back tears and opened her mouth to say it, but she didn't get the chance.

"Please leave." Jess's words were quiet, but final. As if she was trying to hold in her anger, keep from unleashing it on Sadie.

Arguing was a lost cause. Jess wouldn't hear her no matter what Sadie said after that. Sadie had messed up, plain and simple and now she had to face the consequences. There was nothing to do but pull her clothes back on and go. Jess leaned on her dresser, head bent down over it as if she couldn't bear to look at Sadie. She didn't even look up when she left the room.

Sadie didn't allow her tears to fall until she reached the bottom of the stairway. She didn't want Jess to hear her cry. The shock to her system of going from being so intimate with Jess to being told to leave was crushing. Her stomach lurched and her heart ached. She had screwed everything up. She slapped the back of her hand to her mouth to keep the sobs from escaping, and rushed back down the street. Back home.

Once safely inside, Sadie collapsed on the living room couch and let it all out. She cried for being stupid, and she cried for the beautiful moment between her and Jess that she had fucked up. But mostly she cried because she had hurt someone she cared for and broken the trust between them. Because in Jess's eyes she had betrayed her. And that might be something she would never get over.

# CHAPTER TWENTY

Sadie squeezed her eyes shut and tried to lose herself in the beat of the song, but Marley's silky voice kept drawing her focus back to reality. The ladies of Regina Phalange had been in Marley's basement for the past hour and a half rehearsing for their upcoming gig at Lenny's. They were running through the song Sadie had written about Jess. Marley was singing lyrics describing Sadie's very strong feelings about her daughter— now the very strong feelings she was trying to get over.

It had been days of ignored texts and unanswered phone calls. Since Jess had kicked her out of her bedroom four days prior, Sadie had done her damnedest to ram her feelings for Jess back down to a deep, dark corner of her soul where they could wither away to nothingness. The problem was, there was still this small spark of possibility that continued to fight to rekindle the flame that flared when Sadie least expected it, like when she found her Queen of Hearts tank top balled up under her bed where she had tossed it after working that event with Jess. Or the big hot pink bunny in the corner of her bedroom that

Jess had won for her that day at the carnival. The same day that Jess had heard her singing the very song Regina Phalange were rehearsing. *Ugh.*

The words had been true when Sadie wrote them. Since she had been with Jess she had felt a real change in herself. She had shaken off the weight of her past with Corey and the heartbreak of Sugar Stix breakup. She had finally felt her old self waking up somewhere inside her—the Sadie she was before she went to New York, back when she was excited about heading out into the world to make music. Maybe it was something about being back home or performing with a new band, but Sadie suspected the real reason for it was Jess. She brought a joy Sadie had been missing back into her life. With that one stupid mistake Sadie had blown it all. Everything between them was ruined.

Marley continued to croon, *I'm much more me when I'm with you.*

Tears tingled at the back of Sadie's eyes and she swallowed hard against them. She missed a beat and totally lost the rhythm of the song. Her slip-up threw off the whole group.

With the last note she sang still hanging in the air, Marley spun around to face the drum set. "Okay, no problem. We'll take it from the top. Sadie, count us in."

Sadie's arms hung at her sides, her sticks defiantly still. "You know, I think we should scrap this song. It's not working."

"Not working?" Marley's face twisted in confusion. "We flubbed it once. It happens. It's a beautiful song and we've done it right a dozen times. We'll do it again. Count us in."

"No." Sadie's voice came out with more force than she intended and she flicked her gaze down to the drums in front of her, unable to look Marley in the eye. "I mean, this song doesn't work with our set. It doesn't feel like Regina Phalange. It's off-brand."

"Off brand?" Sadie's mom joined in the discussion as she set her guitar in its stand and took a step toward her. Her expression had taken on that hard-set jaw, get-it-together look she would use back when Sadie was a teenager and needed to be reeled back in. "What do you mean *off-brand*, Sadie? We don't need a brand. We need enough songs to get through this gig."

Sadie shook her head. She was the only one in the group who had experience with this type of thing. They didn't understand what she meant by branding. That had to be why everyone was looking at her like she had grown a second head. But she could steer the band right. "Going forward, Regina Phalange has a reputation to keep up. A vibe. And this song—"

"Sadie." Her mom held up a hand to stop her, but her voice was gentle. "There is no going forward for Regina Phalange. We've had fun doing this, and we're excited to play this second show at Lenny's, but that's it. These ladies all have regular lives to get back to."

Sadie's heart sank as she looked from one member of the group to the next, each one nodding in agreement. It made sense that this wasn't a long-term gig for the rest of them. Marley and Sophie had their businesses to get back to. Kristen had her children. Everyone else was on the same page. Everyone else was done with Regina Phalange except Sadie. It was clear there was no point in arguing. Regina Phalange was nearing the end of her reign. Words escaped her as she bit back the sting of tears and surrendered. "Okay."

Sophie and Kristen seemed to busy themselves with their instruments, but her mom approached Sadie and slid an arm around her shoulders, making the threat of tears even stronger.

Mercifully, Marley broke up the awkwardness. "Ladies, let's call it a day. We know our stuff. We're ready for tomorrow."

Sadie swallowed hard and nodded in agreement, not trusting herself to speak without breaking out in sobs. First she lost Jess, then Regina Phalange. It was more than she could take. The band was ready for Lenny's; she knew that. What she didn't know was what she was going to do after that.

# CHAPTER TWENTY-ONE

Jess kicked her running shoes against the retaining wall on the side of the house knocking off clumps of mud that had caught in the tread. It was a problem she had been having the past few days since she had changed her daily run from her old path through the streets of the neighborhood to a new one on the trails through the woods. A small price to pay to avoid the awkwardness of running up and down the street past the DuChamps' house and potentially coming face-to-face with Sadie.

She didn't want to see Sadie, didn't want to hear Sadie, hell, she didn't even want to read the words in the dozens of texts Sadie had sent her since Saturday. How could any of it make up for the way Sadie had betrayed her? Taking the photo was one thing, but then lying about it—that had been the part that pushed Jess over the edge. She had never trusted anyone with the story about her mom's past, but she had let Sadie in. What a huge mistake.

More than anything else, Jess didn't want to go to the show and face Sadie in her Regina Phalange rock goddess moment.

She wanted to be supportive of her mother and her friends, but she had no desire to witness the other patrons fawning over the sexy drummer who used to be hers. Her stomach flopped at the thought of it. *No fucking way.*

Jess kicked the wall one last time—hard enough to send a jolt of pain shooting through her big toe. She hopped back with a yelp and cursed. Locking her hands behind her head, she sucked in a deep breath and attempted to calm down. A big drink of water and a hot shower would probably do her a world of good. But as she entered the house through the sliding door, she found her mother in the kitchen staring at her phone and tapping her nails against her teeth. A sure sign something was weighing heavily on her mind.

"Everything okay?" Jess and her sore toe hobbled over to the fridge to grab a bottle of water.

Her mom gave a frustrated growl, dropped her phone onto the island countertop, and rubbed her fingertips against her temples. "I've been trying for months to get a Queen of Hearts promo night at Watering Hole and now a slot has suddenly opened up."

"That sounds like good news," Jess said between gulps of water. She applied the cold bottle to her forehead and leaned back against the counter. "So what's with the stressed-out face?"

"The slot is tonight." Her mom threw her hands in the air as if all hope was lost and she had no choice but to accept that end times were near. "Tonight. While we're all supposed to be at Lenny's. Like I can just slap an event together."

A last-minute Queen of Hearts event was the perfect excuse for Jess to bow out of going to the show at Lenny's. If she wasn't at the show, she wouldn't have to face Sadie. All she had to do was convince Shanna to do it too, and Jess figured after the past couple weeks of dragging Shanna's drunk ass around, that girl owed her one. She took another big swig of water and made up her mind. "I can. Shanna and I can do it."

Marley shook her head. "Shanna? She's been half-assing her work duties all summer. What makes you think I can count on her now?"

Jess set down her water and placed a reassuring hand on her mother's shoulder. "I got this, Mom. You focus on rocking the house with the ladies at Lenny's. I'll kick Shanna in the pants and handle things at Watering Hole." She rolled her eyes at her mother's doubtful expression. "I'm serious. I got this."

Jess kissed her mom on the cheek before zipping out of the kitchen and up the stairs to hit the shower, suddenly feeling a lot lighter than she had moments before when she was kicking that wall. Compared to facing Sadie in all her rock 'n' roll glory, an impromptu night of handing out vodka and keychains with seldom-sober Shanna sounded like a walk in the park.

# CHAPTER TWENTY-TWO

Sadie blinked at her reflection in the mirror and rubbed her thumb under her eye to touch up her smoky eye makeup. The ladies' room in Lenny's Pizza Place wasn't the ideal green room, but the ladies of Regina Phalange made the best of it. With less than twenty minutes until they were to take the stage, Sadie and her mom were the last two in the little lounge for preshow preparations.

As she shoved her belongings back into her cosmetics bag, she caught a glimpse of her mother beside her. Her mom was applying candy apple red shimmer gloss to her puckered lips and batting her eyelashes at herself in the mottled glass of the mirror. The sight made Sadie's shoulders relax and her cheeks soften into a smile. When her mom stepped back from the mirror and shook her hair out, Sadie couldn't keep her giggle in. "Looking good, Mom."

A bright red smile lit up her mother's face. "If your dad could see me now."

"No kidding." Sadie's heart felt as if it were growing a size or two. It was a relief to see her mother finally looking like her old self. Well, her old self with a rocker chick edge and a bit more makeup. She stepped closer and put a hand on her mom's shoulder. "You look amazing. Totally rock 'n' roll." She hesitated before continuing, not wanting to break the spell. "And this is the first time I've seen you smile while talking about Dad since I've been home."

Mom's expression sobered a bit and she covered Sadie's hand with her own. "I think he'd be quite proud of me tonight. I miss him so, so much. But I know he would want me to keep being me—to still have adventures." She shook her head and blew out a long breath. "Grief is a hell of a thing. It's given me a real run for my money, that's for sure. But the one thing I've learned, and had to accept, is that grieving is a process. There are no shortcuts. You have to work your way through it. I know I'm not there yet, Sadie, but I also know I *will* get there."

Hope swelled in Sadie's chest as her mom turned to face her. "You're going to be okay?"

"Oh, honey, I'm going to absolutely be okay." She wrapped her arms around her daughter. "You don't have to worry about me." She pulled back and studied Sadie's face. Her eyebrows scrunched up in concern. "But I'm a little worried about you. You're about to take the stage and do your most favorite thing in the whole world, so what's with the sad eyes? Is this about Jess?"

Sadie's shoulders sunk and she dropped her gaze down to her well-worn Docs and their stark contrast to the pale yellow, square-inch tiles that covered the bathroom floor. She could put on her tough chick rock 'n' roll act all she wanted, but her mom could still see through it. There was no sense in holding it in. She peered up through her fake lashes at her mom again and confessed, "Tonight is bittersweet for me. I love rocking out like this and I've missed playing in front of people. But this is the last hurrah for Regina Phalange, you know? What's become of my music career? It's like, gone. And on top of that, Jess isn't even here." Sadie squeezed her eyes shut. She couldn't let tears fall and ruin her makeup. She wouldn't take the stage with a voice choked up with sobs. "I guess it's a little bit about Jess."

"Oh, honey."

"No." Sadie shook her hands in front of her and took a step backward, wincing as she bumped her hip against the sink behind her. That was going to leave a bruise. "It doesn't matter. Jess will be back at school in a month anyway I should have never gotten involved with her. I should have spent the summer figuring out what I'm going to do with my life here in Tucker Pointe now that my music career has tanked." She turned away unable to both look her mom in the eye and keep the tears at bay.

"Hey, your career didn't tank." Her mom put a gentle hand on her shoulder and gave it a squeeze. "You had a little setback, but you're twenty-one years old with your whole life ahead of you. You're only getting started."

"I don't know that being a waitress at Lenny's Pizza is much of a start." Sadie tried to joke, but her mom's face didn't reflect humor.

"Sadie, I appreciate you coming home and everything you've done for me, but I raised you to fly like your blackbird there." She nodded at the tattoo on Sadie's upper arm. "I think it's time for you to get back to chasing your dream—whether that be music…or Jess."

"Don't you need me here with you, Mom?"

Her mother pressed her lips together to form a straight line and put her hands on her hips full on authoritarian. "No. What I need is for you to get back to your own life. I need you to thrive, not wither away here with me. You don't have to be here for all of my new adventures. I'll keep you apprised, even if you're back in New York or somewhere else."

A hopeful bubble rose in Sadie's chest. Her mom was telling her to fly, not hunker down in Tucker Pointe. If her mom didn't need her to stick around, she could plan where her music career would go next. Maybe Kellie would have a lead in New York for her. Maybe she would start her own all women band. Sweeter Than Sugar had a nice ring to it for a band name. She could write original songs like the one she wrote for Jess…

Sadie sighed and picked at the frayed edge of a hole in her jeans. "The music I can go back to, but Jess?" She shook her head. "I really messed that up."

Her mom slid her hand down her arm to clasp their hands together. "You made a mistake. If you love that girl, then fix it."

"It's not that easy."

"Of course it's not easy." Her mom pulled a mother-daughter role reversal and rolled her eyes hard. "Nothing worth it ever is. Communication is the key here. You girls need to talk this through."

Maybe her mom was still working through her grief, but her strength-bolstering support of Sadie was as steadfast as ever. She definitely had her mom spark back, and that was a very good sign.

"You really think we'll be able to do that?"

"I think if there's truly something between you, Jess will want to work it out as much as you do. She's had some time to calm down. She's probably missing you too."

Picturing the hurt etched across Jess's face when she asked her to leave that day, Sadie wasn't certain her mom was right about that last part. But she knew if she didn't at least try to get Jess back, she would regret it forever. She squeezed her mom's hand, swallowed hard, and nodded. "I'll do it. As soon as we're done here tonight I'm gonna try my damnedest to get her back."

"That's my girl. Now let's go bring the house down."

Hand in hand, mother and daughter left the restroom, ready to take the stage. But as they stepped into the dining area, Sadie recognized a familiar figure hunched over the bar. She had forgotten that she'd invited Corey and his buddy to witness Regina Phalange's last show. She wasn't convinced his offer to join his band was the fresh start her career needed, but she should at least be polite and say hello. "Hey Corey, are you okay?" As she stepped closer she discovered the reason for his slumped posture. In front of him on the bar were two empty shot glasses and a half empty beer. "What the hell are you doing?"

Corey didn't look up. "I've had a rough night."

"A rough night is a crap excuse to blow your recovery."

The guy on the barstool next to Corey let out a snort and choked on his drink. "Recovery? Man, what kind of bull did you pull on her?"

"Fuck off, Gary," Corey hissed. "I'm laying off the hard stuff."

Heat rose in Sadie's cheeks, embarrassed that she had trusted Corey again. She had fallen for his lies one more time. "You should be laying off *all* the stuff. You're an addict, Corey. God, you'll never change."

"Get off your high horse, Sadie," Corey snarled. "You haven't exactly been honest either, have you?"

Sadie blew out an exasperated breath. "What the hell are you talking about?"

He jerked his head in the direction of the stage. "That's really Rikki Snow, isn't it? Right there in the flesh. Same as she was in that picture you had at your house. I'd know that freaky, filthy slut anywhere."

Sadie's hand slapping his face was as much a shock to her as it was to Corey. "I told you before you are mistaken." She bit out through gritted teeth. "That's my friend. She's not who you think she is. And if I ever hear you talk about her like that again, I swear to god…" Her threat hung in the air. The reality of why Marley tried so hard to keep a low profile hit her full force. Screw being polite. She didn't need to hear any more from her ex. She spun on her heel to walk away, but Corey grabbed her arm.

"Listen, Sadie." He released her when she rounded on him, flinching as if he thought she might hit him again. He grabbed his beer and took a fortifying swig. "I meant what I said earlier. My offer stands if you change your mind about joining the band. We'll take you back to New York with us."

"Yeah," Corey's friend Gary chimed in. "Drummers are a dime a dozen, but from what Corey tells me, your songwriting is the real prize. We could really use you."

Sadie flicked her gaze back to Corey and watched with disdain as he sucked down the last of his beer while simultaneously signaling the bartender for another. No matter how badly she wanted to get her music career back on track, she would never go anywhere with Corey again. She had been foolish to believe he was being honest with her. Corey had taken enough from her when they were a couple and it was time to leave him behind for good. "I'm gonna pass on that. Now if you'll excuse me, I've got a show to play and you two need to get your asses the fuck out of here."

# CHAPTER TWENTY-THREE

Jess poured another tray of vodka sample shots and surveyed the crowd at Watering Hole. The music was loud and the party was in full swing, but her heart was not in it. None of the Queen of Hearts events that summer had lived up to that very first one she worked with Sadie, even if the two of them had ended up in the lake at the end of that night. Remembering that look they'd shared when they both came up from the water, sopping wet in their Queen of Hearts tanks, still made Jess flush warm any time it popped into her mind. But tonight the memory made the blood in her veins run cold. The hard fact was she would never share a look like that with Sadie again. The sooner she learned to accept that, the better off she would be.

She wiped her hands on the bar towel tucked into the waist of her black miniskirt and blew the wisps of hair that hung down from her messy bun out of her eyes with a sigh. Try as she might, she hadn't been able to relax and let loose with the rest of the partiers at the club. She'd done her part—slapped a big, fake smile on her face and mixed and mingled with the crowd while handing out Queen of Hearts swag. Shanna, on the other hand, had been a total star, flirting with patrons and charming the bar staff, and although she hadn't gone full out teetotaler, she wasn't doing her sloppy drunk act either. The change was probably due to the parameters of behavior Jess had set when she roped Shanna into the event. She'd said to her sternly, "You owe me for all the times Sadie and I saved or covered your ass this summer."

Apparently it had worked. That should have done something to set Jess's mind at ease, but instead she had a crawl-out-of-your-skin, icky feeling she couldn't shake, like she was forgetting something, or missing something, or more likely, missing *someone*.

She missed Sadie; there was no denying it. She let out another bone-rattling sigh, this time giving in to the accompanying shoulder slump as she let her head drop to her chest.

"What the hell do we have going on over here?" Shanna slid up behind Jess and poked a finger into the small of her back, startling her into straightening her posture. "Someone has their sad face on. Good thing I came along just in time to put a smile on that mug." Shanna bumped her hip into Jess's and waggled her eyebrows at her.

Jess squinted her eyes and glared at Shanna as she shrugged out of hip's reach. "Shanna, please do not start with me."

"No worries, Jess, I got the message loud and clear the last time. No gal pal sexy times for Shanna and Jess. You don't have to beat a dead horse about it. Wait a minute." She covered her mouth with her fingertips and rolled her eyes up to the ceiling as if searching for an answer there. "I think that phrase is considered politically incorrect these days. It's insensitive to horses. I meant to say, you don't have to feed a dead horse about it."

"Why the hell would someone feed a dead horse? Shanna, are you trying to say something?" Jess spat, her patience shot.

"I'm saying I understand. You and Sadie are all lovey dovey and I am keeping my hands to myself." Shanna eyed the guy sitting at the corner of the bar. "Or maybe on that Hottie McHotterson."

Jess rested her elbow on the high cocktail table they were using for their Queen of Hearts display and dug the pointy heel of her shoe into the laminate floor beneath her. Sadie was no longer an excuse for her hands-off policy with Shanna and the mere mention of that made Jess's heart squeeze with a sadness that must have shown on her face.

"Seriously." Shanna pushed. "What is up with you tonight?"

Jess toyed with the pile of key fobs on the table, reluctant to overshare with Shanna. They had been closer in summers past, but it had been very different this year with Shanna boozing it up and still living the "do 'em and dump 'em" life while Jess had settled in for the season with Sadie. Of course, the weirdest part of all was how Jess didn't miss that old lifestyle at all. She did, however, miss Sadie. "Do save your hands for Mr. McHotterson, but don't do it for Sadie's sake. We broke up."

"Whoa, whoa, whoa." Shanna dragged a barstool up to the table and climbed on, settling in to focus her attention on Jess. "You broke up? Sadie *dumped* you?"

Jess shook her head. "I did it."

"Wait. You finally meet the kind of girl who changes you for the better, a girl who rocks your world, and you let her get away?" Shanna smacked her palm to her forehead dramatically. "I'll ask again. What is wrong with you?"

Heat rose in Jess's cheeks and she scrubbed her face with her hand. "She took something of mine and I got mad about it. I guess I kind of lost my temper and—"

"Sadie stole from you?" Shanna scrunched up her face, incredulous at the thought. "That doesn't sound like her. I did not see that coming."

"She didn't steal it, really. I actually caught her returning it." Jess felt a weird need to defend Sadie before her anger kicked back in. "She had some lame excuse about how she didn't mean to take it."

"So Sadie accidentally borrowed something—and returned it—and that made you angry." Shanna cocked her head, and regarded Jess with a laser-sharp glare. "I don't get it."

"It's not that simple." Jess rubbed her earlobe and bit the inside of her cheek, choosing her words with caution. She would not share her mother's story with anyone else—not after it had gone so wrong with Sadie. "It was something that was important to me."

Shanna slid a hand across the table and placed it gently on top of Jess's, stilling her from rifling through the key fobs. "More important than working things out with the woman you love?"

"I didn't say I was in love with her." Not out loud, anyway, but her heart ached with the truth.

A snort of laughter escaped Shanna. "Honey, I've been hanging out with you all summer. You didn't have to say it."

Jess sucked in a deep breath. Why were her feelings so transparent to everyone else, but it took a smack in the head like losing Sadie for Jess to be aware of them herself? Shanna had made a good point: Sadie had been trying to return the picture and Jess didn't really give her a chance to explain. And the photo was just that—a piece of paper from long ago. She shouldn't miss out on what could be the love of her life because she was too intent on clinging to the past.

That's what Sadie had the potential to be—the love of Jess's life.

"Oh, my god." Jess lifted her gaze to meet Shanna's knowing one. "I…I love her and she's going through something tonight—giving up something that's become very dear to her—and I'm not there for her because—"

"Because you're here." Shanna nodded.

"Because I was too damn stubborn to see the good thing that was right in front of me." *And too afraid to open my heart and trust someone.* She glanced around the club and her stomach clenched. Patrons were buzzing around, having a good time and the night was in full swing, but for Jess it suddenly felt like a prison of her own making. She had volunteered for the event as a way to avoid Sadie, and now there was nothing more in the world she wanted than to be with her. Tears stung at the corners of her eyes. "By the time we get out of here, Sadie's last gig with Regina Phalange will be long over. I'll have missed the whole thing. I really fucked this up, didn't I?"

"Yeah, you did." Shanna slid off her barstool and straightened her skirt. "But it's not too late to set this right. Get your ass to Sadie's show and tell her how you feel."

"I can't do that." Jess shook her head and blinked hard against her swelling emotions. "I promised my mom I'd oversee this event. I can't bail."

"You did oversee the event." Shanna shrugged. "Setup is the part that really needs two people, and we've already started handing out shit." She gestured at the swag on the cocktail table. "I can take it from here."

"What about packing up at the end of the night?"

"The boxes will fit in the back of my car and I'll recruit some muscle from the bar staff." She cocked an eyebrow at Jess, daring her to argue.

Jess regarded Shanna with her crossed-arms stance, challenging her to chicken out on the gift of a second chance. Shanna hadn't exactly been the most reliable coworker lately, but she used to be, and she had come through when Jess had needed her. Shanna had showed up on time, worked with a smile on her face, and remained sober while doing it. Jess's lack of trust in people hadn't served her well as of late. Maybe it was time to reconsider that policy and take a leap of faith. If she didn't, there was a chance she'd never get Sadie back, and that was an outcome she didn't want to face. "Are you sure you got this?"

Shanna placed a gentle hand on Jess's shoulder. "I've got this."

The thump of the music from inside the bar greeted Jess with a pound to her chest the second she jumped out of her Jeep. She navigated the gravel parking lot as quickly as she could in high heels, trying her best not to bemoan her distant spot in the lot. A lot of cars meant a big crowd had turned out to hear Regina Phalange and that was a good thing.

Stepping inside the bar confirmed that suspicion. She paid the cover to the bouncer and pushed through the crowd to find a spot to stand that gave her a good view of the stage. Regina Phalange was rocking through a classic eighties ladies' anthem and the audience was eating it up. Looking hot as fuck in her Regina Phalange T-shirt and driving the beat was Sadie, proving she was as much a rock star as ever. Beads of sweat ran down her face, and her sexy, toned arms flexed and popped as she moved along to the rhythm of the song. A tingle moved downward in Jess's core and her heart skipped a beat. She knew in that instant she had made the right choice by coming to the show. She would take this Hail Mary shot at getting Sadie back. Go big or go home.

The song came to an end, the last notes engulfed in an explosion of applause and hoots from the crowd. As she added her own voice to the roar, Jess realized her mom had caught her from the stage staring at Sadie. Heat rose in her cheeks and she lifted a hand to give a sheepish wave. A grin spread across her mom's face and she gave Jess an encouraging wink, then quickly turned to Sadie at the back of the stage.

This was it. While the band was jamming out that last song, Sadie had probably been too preoccupied to notice Jess's arrival. With Mom pointing it out to the drummer, Jess had to brace herself. This *could* go well, or it could go very, *very* badly. Remembering her own harsh words and the stricken look on Sadie's face the last time they spoke, Jess knew there was a damn good chance it would be the latter. She sucked in a deep breath as her mom returned to the front of the stage and grabbed her microphone from the stand. Sadie's expression was impossible to read—her head was down, eyes focused on her drum set as she adjusted her own mic.

But Jess was jolted out of her thoughts as someone bumped into her shoulder hard enough that she had to side step to keep her balance. "What the hell?" she growled, but the lanky guy didn't even spare her an apologetic glance.

"That has got to be her," he mumbled and staggered toward the stage. "I can't stand it. I have to know if that's Rikki Snow."

Jess's insides lurched as the meaning of his slurred words registered. The very thing she'd worked to avoid for so long was happening. Someone had recognized her mom as Rikki Snow.

And worst of all, she was panicking. Instead of doing something to help, her feet felt like they were suddenly made of lead and she was stuck in place unable to do anything but stare as the scene unfolded in front of her.

The guy cupped his hands around his mouth to amplify his voice. "Rikki? Rikki Snow?"

She caught her mom's deer in headlights expression as the cheers of the audience died down and their attention shifted from the stage to the drunken man pushing through them.

"That's Rikki Snow, the porn star! I could see it in her eyes when I called her name. Damn, I've seen like, all her movies." His gleeful tone dropped as he pointed toward the stage and roared like a madman. "You lied to me, Sadie, you fucking bitch! That singer is Rikki Snow. She's a porn star, not a rock star."

Jess's head swam. Who the hell was this guy and how did he know Sadie? On stage the color drained from Sadie's face, leaving her looking small and frightened. Jess recalled the night she'd spoken of her abusive ex. Corey. *That's Corey!* He was there in Tucker Pointe and he'd exposed her mom's past in front of everyone. Was he going to hurt Sadie now too? *Fuck no.*

That was the thought that rousted Jess to action. She had to stop this guy before things went any further. She rushed forward, planning to tackle his scrawny bod to the ground, but just before she pounced, Michael stepped in front of her. As she bounced to a halt against his broad back, she caught one last glimpse of her mom under the stage lights, her eyes brimming with concern, and Jess knew exactly what was running through her mind. *How would her friends react to hearing the truth about her past?*

Corey's accusations hung awkwardly in the air and throughout the crowd heads swiveled from him to the women up on stage. It was Sadie's mom who finally stepped up to her mic and spoke to cut the tension in the room.

"Anybody in here NOT have a past?" Jennifer's voice was strong and confident as she stood up for her friend.

There was a lot of grumbling and a little shuffling of guilty feet, but no one seemed to have an answer.

"Do you still want to hear us play?" Sophie asked.

The crowd burst into enthusiastic cheers and the women took up their instruments, apparently unfazed by the Rikki Snow revelation.

Jess's heart started beating again as her mom stood straight and proud and grabbed her microphone. "Michael, get this jerk out of here. We've got a set to finish."

With Michael escorting Corey to the exit the color had begun to return to Sadie's face, and Jess let out an encouraging, "Whoop!" Marley's past had been exposed and the world was still turning.

"Ladies and gents, we have a treat for you tonight," Marley addressed the crowd. "As you know, normally I sing the songs. Before that interruption our drummer Sadie told me she wants to sing this one for all of you. Although I think she mostly wants to sing it for one of you in particular." She threw her guitar strap over her shoulder and turned to face Sadie. "Show them what you've got, hon."

Sadie gave Marley a nod, adjusted the height on her microphone stand, and breathed in a deep breath of warm, pizza parlor air. This was her chance. She had said she was going to do her damnedest to get Jess back, and then the opportunity ended up walking into the bar during Regina Phalange's set. She wanted to tell Jess how she felt now more than ever.

She bit her bottom lip and scratched at the back of her head, wavering for the briefest moment in her decision to pour her heart out in front of an audience. Jess's arrival was a good sign, but after everything that had just happened with Corey and Marley, would she be ready to hear what Sadie had to say to her?

Closing her eyes, she took a deep, centering breath. As she released it, she imagined all of her nervous energy draining down through her body and exiting from her toes—an old trick from when she had first started performing in public spaces. It wasn't the audience she had to fortify herself against this time. This was something so much more. It was her big shot at making her feelings clear to Jess and she was counting on her other love—her music—to help her express how much she wanted and needed her. The music would buoy Sadie and carry her through this moment the same as it had with all the other big moments in Sadie's life, only this time it was something even more powerful—the song of her heart. Pausing with the mic in front of her, she opened her eyes, locked her gaze on Jess, and counted the slow, soul shaking tempo of the song she had written for the woman she fell in love with.

*One, two, three, four....*

The words came straight from Sadie's heart. She kept her gaze trained on Jess as she transitioned to the chorus. Jess's expression had been the picture of surprise at the first few bars of the song, but as Sadie sang the lyrics crafted just for the two of them, her bewildered look melted and her face reflected peace and understanding. They both had made mistakes, but there was room for them to heal the hurt. Based on the way Jess pushed through the crowd to come up to the edge of the stage, she was feeling it too.

With you, I'll take the chance
With you, my life's a dance
Without you I don't know what I'd do
I'm much more me when I'm with you
I'm much more me...I'm much more me
I'm much more me when I'm with you

As Sadie sang the last notes of the song, goosebumps ran up her arms and her pulse pounded in her ears. Usually she wished a set would go on forever, but for the very first time she was aching for the music to fade so she could finally take Jess in her arms again.

The crowd broke into cheers and applause, and before Sadie even had time to react, Jess hopped up on the stage and was by her side, pulling her up from her stool.

"That was amazing." Jess took Sadie's hands in hers.

"I meant every word." Sadie gasped, flushed with the excitement of the moment, catching her breath from the performance. "I'm sorry about taking the photo. I should have been honest with you from the start instead of trying to sneak it back into your room. And, God, Corey showing up here…I told him to leave. I thought he had. I'm so sorry."

"No. What he did wasn't anything you could control. I'm just glad you're okay." Jess shook her head. "Besides, I'm sorry for the way I reacted to everything. I didn't even give you a chance to explain about the photo. And now it all seems so stupid anyway. The only thing that matters is that I have you in my life. I love you, Sadie."

"I love you, Jess." Sadie's chest was so full with love she thought she might pop like an overinflated balloon. "And I'd really, really like to kiss you now."

The rest of Regina Phalange continued onto a cover of Iko Iko, the last song of their set with Kristen picking up with the tambourine to keep the beat, but Sadie only had one thing on her mind, and for once that one thing wasn't rock 'n' roll. She took Jess's face in her hands and kissed her deeply and purposely, sealing the deal that they belonged to one another as the band played and the audience cheered, and the curtain went down on Regina Phalange's last show.

# ONE MONTH LATER

Sadie gasped as they pulled up to the valet station outside the hall where the twentieth anniversary gala was being held. The entrance was flanked by a double set of eight-foot-tall playing cards, all in the same suit—the Jack, the King, and on either side of the doorway, the Queen of Hearts.

Jess put the Jeep into park, slid out of the driver's side, and rushed around to open Sadie's door for her. Her braids were the perfect look to go with the neat cut tuxedo she had selected for the evening. She wore her shirt collar open and tieless, instead opting for a large solitaire diamond on a silver chain that belonged to her mother as her sole accessory. The pants were a skinny tapered leg cropped at the calf and drew the eye to the sexy, strappy, red heels that completed the outfit. It was the heels that did Sadie in. That peek of slim ankle on Jess's toned legs turned Sadie's insides to Jell-O and made her pussy throb with want.

She took Jess's offered arm as she stepped out of the Jeep, careful to avoid catching her heel on the hem of her cream-colored Greek goddess wrap dress as her foot reached for the pavement. Her jaw dropped as they entered the hall. "Your mom sure knows how to do a theme."

The oversize deck of cards continued into the ballroom along with plenty of greenery dressed up with strings of lights. The effect was a distinct Queen of Hearts croquet garden straight out of *Alice In Wonderland*. It was magical and over the top, and exactly what Sadie had come to expect from Marley's imagination and sense of style.

"She certainly has her moments." Jess paused and surveyed the room as if trying to take it all in.

The leak of Marley's old alter ego had released a lightning storm of Internet rumors, and managing the social media spin had kept Jess hopping for the past month, but in the end she had handled it and the Queen of Hearts brand had come through mostly unscathed. Marley was thrilled and had made Jess an official partner at Queen of Hearts, even though she still had a semester of classes to wrap up.

Jess took Sadie's hand in hers and led her to one of the toile-covered chairs surrounding the table at the head of the ballroom where they joined their mothers, Kristen, and Sophie. Practically a Regina Phalange reunion. But there was no doubt it was one hundred percent Marley's night and she looked radiant as she greeted the girls.

"Well, the two of you are a gorgeous sight." Marley beamed at them. "Now that you're here we can officially get this party started."

Sadie's stomach took an excited tumble as Jess winked at her before addressing the table.

"I'm glad you think so." Jess licked her lips as if she was dry with nerves. "Um, everyone, Sadie and I have news."

Marley let out a whoop then quickly covered her mouth with both her hands and giggled red-faced as she realized she had jumped the gun. It was no secret that she was a fan of Jess and Sadie ending up together. "I'm sorry. Please go ahead."

Jess grinned joyously and her cheeks flushed pink. "Sadie and I have decided…" She paused as Sadie's mom shifted in her seat and leaned forward expectantly. "We're going to, uh…" She glanced over at Sadie for reinforcement.

Sadie was more than happy to come to her girlfriend's rescue. Her heart was ready to beat right out of her chest from holding in their good news anyway. "I'm going with Jess when she returns to school. She's going to finish her degree and I'm going to focus on writing music."

"We're moving in together," Jess concluded.

For the briefest of moments the table was silent, and Sadie and Jess kept their eyes fixed on one another. But then chaos broke out around them as their neighbors cheered and their mothers hugged, all obviously pleased with the girls' announcement.

Jess squeezed Sadie's hand. "I think they're happy for us, rock star."

Sadie beamed back at her. "None of these people are as happy for us to start our life together as I am, babe. I love you, Jess."

"I love you too, Sadie." Jess pulled her into her arms and onto her lap.

And right there with their family and friends cheering, and Sadie's heart ready to burst with excitement for whatever came next, she kissed the woman she would undoubtedly write songs about for the rest of her life.

Bella Books, Inc.

*Women. Books. Even Better Together.*

P.O. Box 10543
Tallahassee, FL 32302

Phone: 800-729-4992
**www.bellabooks.com**